Nain Rouge:
Book II: The Red Tide

by josef bastian
illustrations by bronwyn coveney

"Nain Rouge: The Red Tide" Copyright © 2013 Josef Bastian
All rights reserved
Illustrations by Bronwyn Coveney Copyright © 2013
ISBN: 978-1484196724
Printed and bound by Booksurge Publishing
Body text in 12-point Arno Pro with 18-point lead.
Chapter titles in 25-point Blackadder ITC.
Cover design and book layout by Carl Winans
First printing.

Stories to be shared.

Honi soit qui mal y pense

(Accursed be a cowardly and covetous heart)

"Nae Man Can Tether Tide Nor Time."

- *From the Statue of Robert Burns in Midtown Detroit*

Prologue.

I**sn't it interesting** how just when one story ends another seems to begin? As the Folkteller, this happens to me a lot. Just when I think that the story I'm sharing with you is over; suddenly another one begins – and we're drawn back together again.

Well, the Nain Rouge has that quality about him as well. Lutin, that's his real name, is the type of creature that lingers on, long after he's disappeared and gone away. Evil seems to work that way. You always have to keep your eye on it because you can never be too sure where it will pop up or what it will do next.

It's true that I've returned to you for a reason, and that reason is to share another story about the Nain Rouge with you.

If you're ready, we'll pick our story up a little further down the road…

Chapter 1
A New Beginning

***I**t was hard to believe* that the school year was more than half over. Winter had washed over the city like a thick, cold ocean wave, ebbing and flowing below the frozen shoes that moved swiftly along the all too vacant streets.

Elly and Tom had made it through the first half of their

freshman year at Royal Oak High School - barely. The high school was such a big change from their middle school days that both teenagers nearly drowned in the overwhelming size of the school, the number of kids and the variety of classes that they were in.

It was as if their lives were in constant motion now. Elly had signed up for far too many clubs again. Between Drama Club, Yearbook and Forensics, there was barely enough time to get through all of the homework from her honors classes.

Tom found high school to be a challenge as well. He quickly learned that there would be no way for him to breeze through his school work without studying or cracking open a textbook. Tom had gotten mostly B's in the first semester, but that was only through great pain and some last-minute cramming for the big tests.

If Elly and Tom had learned anything from the first half of their freshman year of high school, it was this - life had changed. Gone were the days of just sitting around on Elly's front porch, drinking Pepsi and counting the cars as they breezed by down their quiet, tree-lined side street. It also seemed like it was ages ago, when they were drained of their life on the electric midway by that ancient, crimson creature. They often wondered whether it ever happened at all.

Now Elly and Tom saw each other often but not really at all. They would wave at each other between classes, and chat briefly about nothing when they were surrounded at lunch. But there was little to no time after school or on weekends to get together like they used to do. Time seemed to be speeding up for these young adults, as their worlds expanded and accelerated simultaneously.

The third hour bell rang, and soon the halls of Royal Oak High School were flooded with shuffling, swinging student bodies that flowed out of the classrooms and into the narrow passageways. The noise and commotion, accompanied with the forward energy of teenage inertia, reminded one of a flock of migratory birds, sweeping across the sky in a cluttered, controlled formation.

"Tommy!" a voice rose above the shifting crowd.

Tom looked in the direction of the voice, as he stood by his locker, talking trash with his friends Vic and AJ. He could barely make out Elly's voice above the din, but he knew that it was her.

"Hey El, over here!" Tom shouted.

Elly worked her way back upstream from the power current of student traffic flow, sliding in between backpacks and book bags until she landed directly in front of Tom's locker.

"El," Tom spoke with great familiarity, "You know Vic and AJ don't you? He pointed to the two boys standing on either side of him. El looked at each boy for a few seconds and smiled at them both. Vic and AJ returned the greeting with a silent nod and a shy smirk that seemed to form and stick to most teenage boy faces quite nicely.

Vic and AJ had become a pair of complimentary bookends to Tom since the beginning of the year. Both boys were a little shorter than Tom and they always seemed to be standing on either side of him, sideling up against him like fleshy, flying buttresses against the Cathedral of St. Thomas.

AJ appeared to be a quiet, thoughtful young man, who never said too much, but always conveyed a sense of deep knowing and understanding. His short, curly hair and medium-brown skin were in stark contrast to his jade green eyes. AJ liked to listen to Tom tell stories, though he never spoke about his adventure with the evil red dwarf.

Vic, on the other hand, preferred to go toe-to-toe with Tom Demine. Vic and Tom had become good friends over the past few months, despite their penchant for arguing, roughhousing, and picking each other apart at almost every opportunity. Vic was a lot like Tom in many ways. Both boys were strong-willed and self-assured. They both had their own opinions about things and they were not afraid to express themselves with great volume and force. The biggest difference between them was that Vic was a born leader, an overachiever. Where Tom was content to go with the flow and make the best of his surroundings, Vic was a hard driver who had a vision of how things should be. When he set his sights on something, it was very difficult to stop him from reaching his target. Because he was shorter in stature than a lot of the other boys, Vic more than made up for it with his determination, fearlessness and unwillingness to give in – on anything.

This was probably why the three boys were getting along so well. AJ, Vic and Tom all had something inside each of them that the others lacked.

Before any awkward silences could set in, Elly spoke up, "Hey guys, are you going to the basketball game on Friday? If we win, we will be in state finals!"

"Of course we are going El," Tom replied quickly.

"Yeah, you would have to be some sort of loser or geek to miss that game," Vic shot back glibly.

"Shut-up Vic-tor," Tom snapped and swung his elbow directly into Vic's ribcage. Vic hated when anyone called him by his full name.

"Ow! What the heck did you do that for?!!" Vic yelled as he shoved Tom's elbow away from his midsection.

"Your tone…," Tom replied as he stared Vic down, "That was for your jerky tone. El asked a simple question. You don't have to play "Mr. Cool" with her."

"Geez, OK, sorry," Vic responded, looking quickly up at El and then back down again, feeling a little embarrassed.

AJ broke the brief tension between the other three teens, "Why don't we all go together? We could meet up at my house before the game and just walk over to the field house together."

"I'm up for it if you guys are," Elly responded.

The boys looked at each other and soon their eye contact transformed into bobbing, nodding heads.

"Sounds like a plan," Tom confirmed.

It was settled; they would all meet at AJ's house after dinner on Friday and head off to the game together. It's funny how even the simplest plans can become very complicated very quickly. For some reason, that Friday night would become much less simple than anyone could have planned for or even expected.

Chapter 2
Shadows

***T**he sun set cold* and early on the February Friday before the big basketball game. The Royal Oak Ravens were playing the Cass Tech Technicians from Detroit in the southeastern Michigan Interleague playoffs. The winner of the game would be headed to the state finals in Lansing.

Tom left his house at dusk and headed out to pick up Vic before they made their way over to AJ's house. Vic's house was only a few blocks away, past Waterworks Park. But for some reason, on this particular evening, the trip seemed much longer. As Tom walked along the familiar sidewalks, an eerie feeling came over him. It was as if someone was watching him from all sides. He turned to look over at some bushes, then into the street and then behind a parked car. Nothing... There was nothing there. But still, something, something dark and shadowy seemed to swirl around Tom as he quickened his pace toward Vic's house.

Elly was in her room, getting ready for the game. She had on her black and blue Ravens jersey and was now busy putting black and dark blue ribbons in her hair. For the big games, the school would sponsor "Black-Out" nights, where all of the fans were supposed to wear black shirts to show support for the team. Elly wanted to be sure that she looked just right so that everyone would know whose side she was on.

As Elly sat in front of her mirror, continuing her preparations, she felt a slight, cold breeze coming from the small crack from her opened bedroom window. Her curtains billowed gently, as the frigid February air carried across the room, settling on Elly's shoulders like icy fingers pressing against her flesh. She shivered slightly and got up to close the window, mumbling something about her mother always wanting to air out her room.

As Elly moved toward the window, she too got an eerie, slightly breathless feeling like she was being watched. It was as if the entire mood in the room was slowly transforming from the excitement and anticipation of a Friday night out with her friends into a darker, more sinister sinking feeling that settled in the pit of her stomach.

Elly reached the window with great trepidation. She glanced out on the yard. She could have sworn that she saw a dark shadow sweep across her front lawn, moving first from the hedges and then disappearing behind the elm tree in McCreedy's side yard.

Then it happened – to both Tom and Elly – at the same time…

Tom was frozen on the sidewalk, only a few houses away from Vic's front door.

Elly reached out to shut the slightly-opened window.

They both smelled sulphur. They both heard a faint hissing sound that seemed to build into an otherworldly cackle. Tom and Elly's heads began to spin simultaneously. The dizziness was beginning again, as was that all too familiar feeling of nausea and panic that had dominated their lives barely more than a year ago. The smells, the sounds and the continued caterwauling grew inside their heads, like the storm warning sirens that the city tested on the first Saturday of every month – starting quiet and low and then growing into an ungodly crescendo.

Elly wobbled by the window, barely able to stand. Tom held his head in his hands, trying to shake the noise out of his ears. Both teens fell to the ground, succumbing to the spinning of their brains and the churning of their stomachs. In the moment before they finally fell onto the damp, dewy grass and the soft, beige bedroom carpet, they both, as if in some unifying trance, whispered together,

"Oh no, it's happening again…".

Tom struggled his way up, and off of the sidewalk, like a newborn colt, swaying his way into equilibrium. After rubbing his forehead a few times, he looked around to get his bearings only to discover that he was standing right in front of Vic's house. He stumbled his way to the side door of the house and knocked weakly.

Vic opened the door to discover his slightly disheveled pal leaning against the old milk chute by the side of door.

"What the heck happened to you?" Vic asked half smirking.

"I don't really know…" Tom mumbled as he fell into the hallway, "I must have passed out or something on the way over…"

"Well, don't get too excited, the game hasn't even started yet," Vic joked cautiously.

Tom grumbled quietly, "Yeah, thanks for being so understanding, I.. .I … I guess I'll save it for game time."

With that, Vic grabbed his jacket and gently nudged Tom back out of the door. Both boys scooted down the driveway and north on Crooks Road toward AJ's house.

"Come on man, pick up the pace!" Vic yelled at Tom, who was still lagging behind. "We are already late and everyone is going to leave without us."

"OK, OK," Tom said, making a feeble effort to quicken his steps, "You haven't even given me a chance to tell you what happened back there."

On the other side of town, Elly was slowly pulling herself up off of her bedroom carpet. Fortunately, her head had just missed the corner of the window sill when she collapsed in a heap upon the floor. She propped herself up against the side of her bed and brushed her long brown hair away from her face.

After stabilizing herself, Elly stood up straight and made her way toward the vanity mirror. Despite her sudden fainting spell, she surprisingly looked no worse for wear. Her hair ribbons were a bit askew, but nothing that a little tightening and adjusting couldn't fix. The clock on the vanity table read 6:30pm.

"Oh geez, I better get going!" Elly said to herself, "I hate being the last one to show up at AJ's."

With great speed and precision, Elly finished putting on her make-up and thundered down the stairs.

"Be home by eleven!" her dad yelled to her from the family

room.

"OK, Dad, got it!" Elly yelled back, as her last words slammed in unison with the front door that closed behind her.

In her rush towards AJ's house, Elly almost ran into her friend, Lynni, right on the front porch. Fortunately, Lynni heard the door and saw Elly coming right at her just in time to hold her hands up and slow down the runaway freight train.

"Hey, what's the hurry?!!" Lynni yelled as she pushed Elly back onto the porch.

"Oh Lynni, you startled me!" Elly exclaimed, "I almost forgot that you were going to meet me here."

"Gee thanks, El, and I'm your best friend, right?" Lynni replied, rolling her eyes.

"Oh shut up," Elly shot back, "I just got pre-occupied with something, that's all."

Lynni looked at Elly's face and could see a look of worry. It was a look like she'd never seen before. Whatever had pre-occupied Elly enough to almost knock her best friend off of the front porch had to be pretty serious.

"Alright El, give it up, what is floating around that little head of yours?" Lynni questioned.

Elly looked down at the ground for what seemed like an eternity. She couldn't look Lynni in the eye. She had never told anyone about what had happened two summers ago. And besides, she was probably just over reacting, letting her imagination get the best of her. She needed to talk to Tommy. That would make her feel better. She could clear everything up at AJ's house before the game.

"Nothing," was Elly's response to Lynni, "Let's get going and we can talk on the way. I think I just got over excited about the big game tonight."

With that, Elly took Lynni's arm and the two girls slipped deeper into the February darkness, making their way across frozen lawns and driveways toward the pre-game party.

Chapter 3
The Company Misery Brings

*A*J's house was abuzz with excitement. His parents had let him set up the basement for the pre-game festivities. By the time Elly and Lynni arrived, Vic, Tom and AJ were all relaxing on the futon couch, watching TV and eating Doritos.

AJ's dog was the first to greet the girls as they thumped down the basement steps. Everyone loved AJ's dog, Pippi, who was called "Pip" for short. Pip was a West Highland White Terrier, with big brown eyes and a scrappy, friendly disposition. AJ's mom had named the dog after Pippi Longstocking, a character from a book she had loved as a child. Pippi Longstocking was an independent, strong-willed girl, who lived alone in a crazy house by the ocean, while her sea captain father was away on his ship. Pip the dog seemed to exude a lot of the same qualities as the character from the book. She was willful, smart and full of energy.

Pip jumped up to meet the girls and reveled in the attention. Their high sweet voices and pats on the head made Pip flatten her ears and wag her tail wildly. Pip led the teens over to where the boys were sitting.

"Hey guys!" AJ greeted Elly and Lynni, as they sat down in the two beanbag chairs to the right of the couch.

"Hey, what's goin' on?" Elly replied, slightly uneasily.

AJ whispered, "Well, Vic was just telling me about Tom passing out on the way to his house."

Elly suddenly sat up with complete alertness and panic. She shot a look over to Tom that penetrated right through his heart and into his soul. Tom locked eyes with Elly, knowing that something was not right. The next few minutes seemed to pass like hours between the two of them. Their gaze never broke as they tried to decipher each other's thoughts in the awkward silence of that lingering moment.

Vic finally broke the tension, "OK you two, what the heck is going on? You both keep staring at each other like a couple of zombies."

Lynni added, "Yeah, El, you have been acting weird ever since I got to your house. Now you and Tom are having a crazy-eyed staring contest."

AJ pointed out, "I get the feeling that there's something you haven't told us yet…"

All of this questioning broke the spell. Tom and Elly's stare snapped in half, as they turned away from each other and faced the center of the room again. It was at that moment a deep realization came over the both of them. Despite everything that had happened to them over the past couple of years, they had never told anyone. Not a soul knew about Lutin (the Nain Rouge's real name), the legend, or how close Tom and Elly had come to meeting their doom. Once high school had started, Tom and Elly had gotten so caught up in all of the activities and the big changes that were happening all around them, they had shoved the whole Nain Rouge experience back into the recesses of their minds.

Now, the events that had taken place that night had brought everything back, the fear, the anxiety, the sense of loneliness that had drained them of their life and energy once before. Neither of them wanted to go through that experience again. They couldn't do it, even if they wanted to, they just did not have the strength to deal with all of that bad energy alone.

Tom looked over at Elly with his lips pursed. His eyes questioned her as to what he should say next. Elly returned the knowing look with a reassuring nod of her head that was so subtle, only Tom had noticed it. Elly and Tom were ready to talk. They needed to tell their story.

"Um, you guys probably are not going to believe this…" Tom began, "Actually, El and I have never told anyone about this before."

"What's the big mystery Tom?" Vic quipped, "Are you sick or something?"

Lynni sat next to Elly and turned her head toward her in dramatic fashion, "Oh my gosh El, is everything OK?"

AJ sat there looking around the room at the worried expressions that hung from all of the teenagers' faces. Even Pip the dog sensed that the mood had changed in the room, and began brushing her head gently against the indiscriminate legs that rested on the floor or dangled down from the futon couch.

Tom hunched over from the chair in which he was sitting, leaning into the center of the group. "Guys, there is nothing to worry about. It is just that a lot of weird stuff happened to El and me a couple of summers ago. We never really had a chance to talk to anyone about it. Tonight, when I passed out in front of Vic's house, well, it just kind of brought it all back."

Elly jumped right in the middle of Tom's confession, "Tommy, you fainted tonight?!!"

Tom responded quietly, "Yeah, I got that weird feeling again, like we used to get when, uh, um, when he was around, you know?"

Elly's eyes widened as she stood up with a sick, grave look on her face, "I passed out too, just a few hours ago, in my room. I had the same cold, uneasy feeling - just like before…"

The tension in the room was now even higher. Glances and looks shot around the room like super balls dropped into a clear, plastic cube. Lynni yelled, "Guys, what the heck in going on? We're flippin' out here, wondering what you both are talking about!"

Tom motioned for Elly to sit back down so that he could continue his story.

"Well guys, the reason we never told anyone about everything that happened to Elly and me is that we thought that no one would ever believe us. But now, since this weird stuff is happening again, we need to trust someone. We need to trust all of you."

Tom paused for moment and searched the faces of his new friends. He was looking for any sign of fear, confusion or disbelief before he went any further. As he scanned their eyes, Tom could see that everyone was riveted to what he was saying. They were hanging on each word with a concern and caring that he could never have hoped for, but was really grateful for having.

Tom cleared his throat and continued, "Well, about a year and half ago, Elly and I were on a field trip with the middle school. We were down at the DIA looking at the Diego Rivera murals when we saw something. Actually, we heard something – a something that made a huge noise and knocked over a bunch of knights' armor. Once we saw it, we passed out."

As if in unison, Vic, Lynni and AJ blurted out simultaneously, "What was it?"

Elly answered, "It was the Nain Rouge."

Tom continued, "Nain Rouge is French for 'red dwarf.' After the incident, the curator of the museum, Dr. Hieronymus Beele, took us up to his office and explained that this red dwarf was a harbinger of doom that had been plaguing Detroit for centuries. There was a curse, a curse on the city that we had just gotten pulled into."

Tom took a breath and looked around the room again. All eyes were fixed directly on him and no one said a word. Tom looked a bit winded, and so he directed Elly to pick up the story from where he had left off.

Elly stood up and moved into the center of the group. "Like Tommy said, we were sucked into some ancient curse. We had no idea why all this stuff was happening to us. That was until we did a little research and found out that we were related to some of the original settlers of Detroit. Tommy and I learned that we were the ransom to this curse."

"AJ leaned forward a little and questioned, "How did you find all of this out, from Dr Beele?"

"No," Elly continued, "From the Nain Rouge himself! We actually met this little troll and he told us that he was the product of all the evil that had been building up in the city over the centuries. Since our ancestors tried to kick him off his land when Detroit was founded, he cursed them… and all of their descendants… including Tom and me."

Tom added, "Yeah, he basically tried to kill us, always mumbling this curse:

'Take what you steal and steal what you keep
The shepherd must pay for his sins with his sheep'."

Vic looked over at Tom, leaning his head to one side with an expression of disbelief, "For real? You're kidding right?"

"No," Tom said quietly and gravely, "I wish I was. That red dwarf was slowly sucking the life out of us. We were goners for sure until Elly came up with a really clever plan. She got him to cross over the border of the city, right by the State Fairgrounds during the Freedom Festival. He fell for it and burned up into nothingness. The only thing that was left was a slick puddle of black goo that slid into the sewer.

After all that happened, things seemed to get better, that is until now."

Elly added, "Tommy and I figured that the problem was solved. Then tonight, those old feelings came back. It was as if it was starting all over again…"

With that, Elly broke down and cried. Lynni jumped up and wrapped her arms around Elly, gently guiding her back down to the couch, where Elly buried her face in Lynni's shoulder. "I just can't go through this again, Lynni, I just can't!"

Tom rubbed his forehead roughly with his hand, trying to take in what had happened this evening, along with the powerful memories from the past that were now spinning around his head in endless cyclones of confusion. Vic and AJ got up put their hands on Tom's shoulders.

"It'll be OK, man," Vic said comfortingly.

"Yeah, you're not alone this time," AJ added with thoughtful assurance.

Eventually, the energy in the room settled down, and the teens' emotions ebbed slightly. Tom and Elly were glad that they had shared their adventure with their new friends, even though they had a feeling that their troubles from the past were beginning to resurface.

After a little while, Lynni broke the silence, "You know, we can just hang out here. We don't have to go to the game if you guys don't want to."

"No," Tom replied, "I still want to go, what about you El?"

Elly agreed, "Yeah, let's go. I didn't spend all that time getting ready just to sit in AJ's basement all night."

It was agreed. After a little cleaning and straightening up, the small group of friends headed up from the basement out into the subtle sting of the cold, empty evening. Pip ran after them from the basement, scooting around the teens to stand at attention near the front entrance. AJ tried to shoo the little white dog away as he opened the door. But when AJ opened the main door, Pip pressed even harder against storm door, growling in a low, menacing gurgle at something unseen in the darkness of the evening.

"Wow, she's never growled like that before," AJ said with a bit of concern in his voice.

Pip continued to stand rigid, with her eyes fixed on the blackness that draped over the entire evening.

"Do you think there's something out there?" Lynni asked with trepidation.

Tom interrupted, "OK guys, let's stop spooking ourselves and just go already!"

"Yeah," Elly added, "It won't do us any good to keep hanging around here."

Everyone seemed to agree. It was not like they could hide from what may or may not happen to them. They were going to have to face whatever was out there, if there *was* something out there at all.

AJ scooped up Pip and set her behind the doggie gate in the family room and the team made their way out through the front door. As they closed the door, everyone could still hear the high-pitched "yap" of Pip's warning bark. She was sounding the alarm that something may be lurking in the unknown darkness of a night that was growing stranger by the minute.

Chapter 4
Black Out

***A**s they made* their way up Crooks Road, the teens could hear the muffled roar of the crowd, already packed into the field house. Soon, they would be smack-dab in the middle of the signs, cheers and waving arms that signified the black and blue Ravens spirit.

The visiting side of the Ravens field house was jammed to the rafters with visiting fans from Cass Tech, decked out in green and white. The usual swell of supporters that came to cheer on the Royal Oak Ravens filled up the home side of the arena as the party of teenagers entered the building. Tom, Elly and the rest of the gang made their way over to the student section, blending into the sea of blue and black.

There was a great feeling of electricity in the air, as the players took to the court for the opening tip-off. Both sides moved up and down the court with such great speed and precision that the fans had trouble swiveling their heads in time to catch each block and basket.

Near the end of the second quarter, Elly, Tom and the rest of their friends could hardly speak. They had been yelling so loud, that their voices were hoarse with the non-stop excitement. On both sides of the field house, fans were so absorbed in the game, that no one noticed the overhead lights beginning to flicker – one by one.

Light by light, the arena grew dimmer. As each light faded, it would expand into a blinding brightness. Then suddenly, it would explode in a pyrotechnic display of sparks and shattering glass.

What happened next is still disputed to this very day. Some say they saw a shadowy figure run across the court and out the side doors of the field house as the fans scattered and players ducked their way back into the locker rooms. Others say they saw a wild animal circling the sidelines, growling menacingly as darkness fell upon the arena.

Tom, Elly, AJ, Lynni and Vic knew better. As the lights overhead began to explode, Elly grabbed Tom's arm and pointed toward the ceiling. The rest of the group looked up as Elly motioned skyward. Above their heads, they saw a small troll-like man swinging from light to light. As he touched each light with the tip of his long, pointed finger, the light would fade then expand in an explosive flash that shattered each bulb completely.

"Oh my gosh!" Lynni yelled, "Run!"

"No!" Elly shot back, "That is just what he wants us to do. Follow me!"

With that, Elly led the group to the top of the bleachers, where they huddled together until the chaos subsided. As they sat there, all hunched together, they watched Lutin destroy every light in the arena. Soon, the building was left empty and in complete darkness.

Just before the last light went out, all of the teens' eyes were drawn to center court. In the middle of the blue R.O. emblem, they saw the tiny creature, glowing in an incandescent red, spin gleefully amidst the shards of glass now strewn on the wooden floor. With a final cackle and a deft pirouette, they saw the Nain Rouge evaporate and simply disappear right before their eyes. But just before he disappeared from view, both Tom and Elly could have sworn they heard a low, hissing rasp of a voice whisper in their ears:

"You have done it, children… You have released me…"

Chapter 5
Sorting Things

***E**lly looked over* at Tom from the top of the bleachers.

Tom stared back at her, half in disbelief, half in sickened terror. Vic, AJ and Lynni hadn't moved, still curled up from the darkness and noise that had swallowed them up just a few minutes before.

Tom tapped AJ on the shoulder, "C'mon man, it's OK now. You can get up."

Elly roused Lynni and Vic from their balled-up state, letting them know that they could safely look out from the top of the field house.

Vic was the first to speak, "I guess you guys weren't kidding when you told us what happened to you in middle school."

Tom replied with a dazed and confused look as he looked down at the vacant, glass-covered basketball court, "I just don't get it... How? How could he be back?"

Lynni piped in, "Didn't you guys say that you destroyed him?"

"Yes," Elly replied thoughtfully, "We did. We made him cross over the city limit. That was the boundary that trapped him in the city. It was all part of the curse. He burned up, melted away. There was nothing left but a scorch mark on the sidewalk. I was there, I saw it all happen. I know it wasn't a dream..."

Elly's voice trailed off into the darkness that shrouded the arena. She could not figure out how it had happened. How had Lutin come back? Why was he showing his twisted face outside of the city now?

After the group had regained their senses a bit more, they stumbled down from the top of the bleachers and made their way toward the exit doors. They each tip-toed lightly across the basketball court, carefully avoiding the bigger shards of broken glass as the tiny, shiny bits crunched beneath their feet.

Once outside the building, the teens regrouped by the old oak tree that loomed in shadowy silence just on the outskirts of the school yard. In the distance, they could hear the police and ambulance sirens coming closer. It seemed like they had been huddled inside the field house for hours, when actually it had only been a few minutes since the chaos had passed.

The night had grown a bit darker, a bit colder than when they had left AJ's house earlier that evening. They all knew that they were safe in the shadow of that old tree, just far enough away from the school and just camouflaged enough to remain hidden from the inevitable questions and concerns that would be coming from the police and ambulance personnel.

In the temporary security of their hiding place, the friends attempted to make some sense out of the bizarre events that had taken place that night.

In the silence, each head seemed to turn to where Elly was leaning against the trunk of the great tree. They could see that Elly was deep in thought, recalling events and details from the last time she had run into the red dwarf. She was racking her brain, trying to figure out how Lutin could have escaped.

Elly thought to herself, "Hadn't they broken the curse? Weren't they free from the Nain Rouge's power? How could he be outside of the city? And what was he up to now?" All of these thoughts repeatedly circled and cycled through her mind like the handle of a jack-in-the-box, cranking until the answer popped out suddenly from out of the top of her head.

"I think I've got it!" Elly burst out from beneath the oak tree branches.

"Shhhhh!" the rest of the teens whispered.

Vic added, "Someone will hear us if you keep that up."

"Sorry," Elly whispered in a much lower tone. "I was just thinking... maybe, when we broke the curse, we accidently let him go!"

"What do you mean, let him go?" Lynni questioned.

At that moment, Tom piped in thoughtfully, "El, I think you may be right. Maybe when he crossed over the border of Detroit, it not only broke the curse but released him too! Think about it - Lutin himself told us that he was tied to the land. He was part of the energy of the land and actually became more powerful as the negative energy increased over hundreds and hundreds of years. The curse was the only thing keeping him in Detroit. Maybe, it was the curse that created the boundaries that held him within the city!"

"That would mean that the source of his power was also the source of his confinement," AJ concluded as he hunched close to the trunk of the oak tree.

As the teens huddled together in the shadow of the high school, they notice a strange, cold wind beginning to blow through the leafless branches of the giant oak. As the bitter breeze nipped their cheeks and noses with increasing intensity, a pungent whiff of sulphur mingled with the air, creating a cold, foul smell that made some of them cough and gag.

Through the air, a dark shadow, like a wisp of midnight, filtered down from the sky, slithering through the bare branches of the ancient tree. From directly above the youngsters, a high, raspy voice emanated down from the treetop,

"Clever… children…" the voice hissed.

All heads immediately looked up through the branches to see the Nain Rouge manifesting himself on one of the sturdier boughs of the tree, like an evil Cheshire cat, complete with menacing grin and glowing ember eyes.

"Clever children," he repeated, "You have found me out all too quickly. You've left me little time to thank you for your thoughtful gift of freedom."

"But how?" were the only words that could come out of the teens' mouths. No one was quite sure who had even asked the question as they huddled even closer, staring at the red dwarf that sat so proud and satisfied above their heads.

"Now is not the time for explanations," Lutin stated curtly.

"Suffice it to say that these two were correct in their assumption. The broken curse has set me free," Lutin's voice grew with excitement as he pointed at Tom and Elly.

"Now, I have much to do and little time for dawdling with you pests."

With that, Lutin returned to his smoky form, entwining himself within the branches of the tree. As his elongated body wrapped around the trunk of the tree, a strong gust of wind rose up from the west.

Lynni looked up from the gathered group and yelled, "Run!"

As the children scurried out from underneath the outstretched oak tree, they could feel the power of the wind pulling on the roots of the oak, prying it violently from the ground. Just as the friends pulled away from the shadow of the tree, they heard a great crashing sound like a tornado blowing through a wood-framed farmhouse.

The thunderous crash felt like a freight train rolling off its tracks.

As they all lay on the ground, barely past their outstretched feet, they saw the remnants of the ancient oak, now shattered and splintered all around them. As the wind continued to howl, they could hear a faint, high-pitched cackling in the distance.

Lutin was back.

The year of calm and quiet that had settled into Tom's and Elly's lives disappeared altogether.

Nothing would ever be the same again.

Chapter 6
The New Alliance

One by one, they gathered themselves up, dusted themselves off and began a rapid retreat back to AJ's house. Pip was at the door to greet them, barking and agitated, as if she knew what had happened to them that evening.

The teens flicked on the basement lights and scurried down into their safe haven, flopping with great exhaustion on both the futon and the floor.

Vic was the first one to break the silence, "Man, what a night!"

Tom replied with a bit more calm and worry, "That's just a little taste of what Elly and I had to go through a few years ago… I was hoping that we'd seen the last of Lutin back then…I guess not…"

Lynni wondered out loud, "Do you think anyone saw what happened to us? I mean, we were almost killed!"

"I doubt it," AJ interjected, "We were too far away from the crowd, and besides, people were more focused on the noise and the damage to the gym to notice anything else."

As the group pondered the events from the evening, Elly sat there quietly, as if in deep thought. Her brow furrowed in deep concentration, as she rubbed her temples with her thumb and forefinger, she could not help but wonder…

"What is he up to?" she finally questioned out loud.

Everyone's head turned to meet Elly's questioning, as they had been in deep conversation, rehashing every minor detail of Lutin's reappearance.

Elly continued, "He has to be up to something. He even said that he didn't have time to waste on us. That means he must have more important things on his devious, little mind."

Tom answered her directly, "El, we aren't important to him anymore. The curse is broken, he doesn't need us - he's got his freedom now."

"Then why did he try to kill us?" Vic shot back.

"That's the funny part about it," Elly continued, as if she was still thinking it all the way through, "He could have killed us if he wanted to. Like Tom said, he's not bound by the curse anymore. But he didn't. What he did do was deliberately pull that stunt at the field house. It was for our 'entertainment'. The Nain Rouge wanted us to know that he was back in grand style."

"But what about the tree?" Lynni said, "Wasn't he trying to kill us then?"

"No," Tom replied gravely, "If he had wanted us dead, we wouldn't be here talking about it now. Lutin just wanted us to know how powerful he's become. He wanted to make it clear that he's unstoppable."

"How can you be so sure?" Vic debated.

"Listen guys," said Tom as he leaned forward, sliding his backside onto the edge of the futon couch, "I'm still not sure what's going on here, neither is Elly. All I know is that Lutin is back, we aren't dead and some more bad stuff is going to happen. The Nain Rouge has bigger plans this time, bigger than snuffing out a bunch of freshmen."

It was Tom's directness and clarity that caused a hush to fall over the entire basement. Everyone sat back in their spots and contemplated the gravity of Tom's stark assessment and bold prediction. At least when it was just Tom and Elly, they knew what they were up against. Before, Lutin made it very clear what his intentions were and what Tom's and Elly's fate would be. Once they discovered his intentions, they were able to craft a plan to defeat him.

It was different now. There were more people involved. There was no curse to contain him. Most of all, Lutin revealed nothing to them, only that he was free. That was the worst part about it. It was the not knowing that caused them the greatest fear.

The silence was broken by a faint, mourning sound, like a wounded dove. AJ looked over to see Elly weeping into her hands. Tom pursed his lips when he discovered what AJ had already picked up on, trying bravely to not start crying himself.

There were no words of comfort that anyone could find to console Elly at that moment. Tom and AJ bent down on either side of her and began gently rubbing her shoulders. Tom leaned over and put his forehead against Elly's.

"It's going to be alright, I promise." Tom said softly.

Yeah," AJ added, "You're not alone this time, remember?"

With that, Vic and Lynni joined the others, gathering around Elly in an impromptu group hug. It was true - this time Elly and Tom were not alone. Whether they liked it or not, they had dragged their new friends into one of the most dangerous and exciting adventures of their lives.

No one knew what was going to happen next. All they did know was that they would go through it together. In the years to come, each of them would look back on this moment as a time when they all grew up a little bit.

They would soon learn that troubled times have a strange way of either tearing people apart or bringing them closer together.

Chapter 7
Back to Beele

*A**nother late February** morning broke faintly through the clouds. A feeble sun made an anaemic attempt to lift the gloom of a late winter dawn. Tom stirred from his bed, awakened only by the electric buzz of his alarm clock, sounding the warning that another day of school was upon him.

In other houses around Royal Oak, similar scenes were playing out in the bedrooms of Elly, AJ, Lynni and Vic. Despite their bodies' desire to remain beneath the warmth and security of their cotton comforters, the teens knew that school waited for no one – they would inevitably have to get up. So, with a succession of grumbling, mumbling and inaudible groans, each of them stumbled from their beds and began their unique morning rituals of high school preparation.

AJ tumbled down the staircase like an over-stretched slinky. He made his way into the kitchen, where his mom and dad were already pressed, dressed and ready for another day of work. Pip scooted over to AJ and rubbed her white head against his ankles. Her brown eyes reached way up to AJ's face in anticipation of a breakfast treat or some of his cold cereal that he had begun to pour into his bowl.

"No more Cheerios for her," mom said to AJ, "She's had enough already."

"Did you see the Web News Network this morning?" Dad said as he unfolded his laptop computer. He angled the screen so that both AJ and his mom could see the headlines on the main page of the web site,

"14th Street Bridge Collapses in Washington DC, Dozens Injured."

AJ's dad began to read the first paragraph of the article,

"Late last night, structural supports gave way on the 14th Street Bridge, which connects Arlington, Virginia and Washington DC. Dozens of motorists were injured when the bridge collapsed beneath their moving vehicles, plunging them into the Potomac River.
Sergeant William Edmunds of the DC police noted,
'It was a good thing this didn't happen during rush hour. We could have had a real tragedy on our hands.'
Causes for the collapse remain unknown, though the case is being investigated by both local and federal law enforcement as well as the Army Corps of Engineers."

AJ almost dropped his cereal bowl on Pip's head. There was something about that story that didn't sit right with him.

"Well, I'm just glad no one was seriously injured," Mom said with a deep sigh and a slight shaking of her head.

AJ finished his breakfast quickly. Now he had a really good reason to finish getting ready for school. He was not really sure why, but he had a peculiar feeling that the newspaper headlines and the events from last night had something to do with each other. Either way, he had to meet up with the others to see what they thought.

It was still a few minutes before the first bell, when the teens had gathered around Lynni's locker. AJ came running up to Vic, Tom, Elly and Lynni with a look of such energy and intent, that they all stopped talking, right in the middle of their conversation.

"Did you guys see the news this morning?" AJ blurted out.

"What, was there a story about a tree nearly falling on us?" Vic quipped sarcastically.

"Not funny Vic," AJ stammered, "I meant the story about the bridge collapse in Washington DC…"

Elly and Tom looked at each other with an uneasy feeling.

AJ continued, "I know it sounds crazy, but I just have a feeling, right in my gut, that what happened to us last night and what happened on that bridge are connected in some way."

"That's crazy," Lynni said dismissively. "Disasters happen every day, all around the world. So how does being attacked by a red dwarf in Michigan connect to a bridge collapsing in Washington DC?"

"Now, hold on a minute," Tom stepped in to defend AJ, "I don't know if there is a connection here or not. But I do know that Lutin is capable of pretty much anything. The Nain Rouge is the kind of creature that works his way into your gut as well into as your head."

Elly agreed, "I haven't seen the paper this morning, but as soon as AJ started talking about the bridge, I had that queasy feeling in my stomach too."

Just then the first bell rang.

Tom pulled everyone together before they took off toward their first classes of the day, "Listen guys, we can't prove anything by ourselves. I think we should go talk to Dr. Beele."

"Yes!" Elly exclaimed, "I was going to suggest that just from what happened last night. He at least needs to know that Lutin is back on the prowl."

"Can everyone make it after school?" Tom questioned the entire group. Everyone said that they could make the bus trip downtown to the Detroit Institute of Arts. Tom would call at lunch and make a special appointment to meet with Dr. Hieronymus Stanley Beele, Curator of Art, Antiquities and Keeper of Unknown Knowledge.

The rest of the school day passed slowly and anxiously. Even the afternoon bus ride downtown proved uneventful. After checking in at home, the small band of friends was to meet at the SMART bus station near 12 Mile Road and Woodward Avenue. Elly and Lynni showed up first, since Elly's house was in walking distance to the intersection. The two girls stood there silently in the giant stone shadow of the Shrine of the Little Flower. The Crucifixion Tower drew a cold, dark curtain across the avenue, blanketing both teens with an enduring, foreboding chill that crept into the bus stop waiting station.

"Why do those guys always have to be late? I'm freezing out here." Lynni complained.

"Uh, probably because they're guys, it's their nature." Elly replied coolly.

Just as the words snapped out of Elly's mouth, they saw Vic, Tom and AJ approaching the bus station from across the boulevard. Vic waved his arm vigorously to catch their attention, while the girls stood there with their arms folded, staring back at the boys with frozen looks of impatience.

"What took you guys so long?" Lynni asked with a curt, steely tone in her voice.

"We're sorry," AJ explained, "We all met at my house to come over here. Pip was acting crazy and didn't want us to leave. I tried to put her behind the dog gate but she ran outside after us. Vic and Tom had to help me chase her down to get her back in the house. It was weird; she's never acted like that before. It was like she didn't want us to go, like she sensed that something bad was going to happen."

"Well, I'm glad you caught her, but we've missed seven buses already just waiting for you guys."

"Sorry El," Tom said humbly, "But we're here now and another bus is on its way right now, look."

The boys were fortunate that another bus was heading south toward them. This meant that they could get on the bus, get out of the cold, afternoon air, and minimize the complaining and griping they were sure hear from their miffed counterparts.

Once everyone got on the bus, it made its way down the familiar route, south into the city. On the 20 minute ride, they drove through Royal Oak, Berkley, and Ferndale making frequent stops along the way. The stop Tom and Elly remembered most was near the series of red lights at the intersection of 8 Mile Road and Woodward.

When the hydraulic brakes hissed the bus to a slow stop, Tom and Elly were still caught off guard. They had become so accustomed to the frequent stopping and starting that they had been lulled into a sort of dreamlike state by the white noise of the engine, the conversations between friends and the rumbling movement of their 12 ton vehicle.

Suddenly, there it was, right in front of them. The traffic lights marked the city limit, the entrance and exit to the city of Detroit. Out of the bus window they could see the old state fairgrounds. On the other side of the boulevard, they could see the stone and wrought iron fencing surrounding Woodlawn Cemetery.

"It happened right here…" Tom's voice trailed off into an ethereal, faint whisper, like a ghost struggling to tell the story of its demise.

Vic shook Tom and Elly back into reality, "What are you two babbling about? You're starting to freak me out with the creepy way you're staring out the window!"

The trance was broken and Elly turned her face away from the bus windows toward the group of friends.

"Sorry guys, it's just that, that, well, uh, Tommy and I haven't been down this way since everything happened. I think we kind of forgot about this spot."

"What spot?" Lynni wondered.

"The spot where we battled the Nain Rouge, it was right here at the city limits, "Elly pointed over to a north side corner of the intersection where Woodward Avenue crossed over 8 Mile Road.

"That was right where he burned up and melted," Tom cut in, pointing his finger toward the back of the bus, in parallel with Elly's already outstretched hand.

All of the teens followed the pointing fingers to the spot near the street where Lutin had been destroyed. They could still see a thick black stain on the sidewalk that had faded little in the years that had passed.

As the bus churned through the green light, the kids were pulled back into their seats by the inertia of the forward movement. The dark shadow on the sidewalk pulled out of view and the bus continued its way south toward the DIA. An odd silence seemed to fall over the group once they had crossed into the city. For some strange reason, no one knew what to say as they prepared their individual thoughts and questions for the great and mysterious Dr.

Beele.

Perhaps, it may have been that Vic, AJ, Lynni, Tom and Elly didn't lack for things to say but instead, couldn't find the words to describe the evil they were up against.

Chapter 8
The Curious Curator

The *steps of* the DIA were slick and wet from the snow that had been melting all day in the late winter sun. It was four o'clock and the band of investigators only had an hour to speak with Dr. Beele, before the museum closed and they would have to head back to Royal Oak.

As the teens approached the path up to the main doors of the museum, Tom and Elly stopped dead in their tracks. Directly in front of them loomed Rodin's "Thinker" statue, sitting upon its granite pedestal, staring out onto Woodward Avenue in perpetual contemplation. The memories of the last time they had passed the statue came flooding back.

"What's wrong now?" Lynni approached Elly, following her friend's gaze up upon the statue.

"Nothing, nothing's wrong," Elly responded, "Everything is fine, really."

"It's OK guys," Tom explained, "It's just that the last time we passed this statue, it came to life and tried to kill us – no big deal."

AJ, Vic and Lynni took a long, slow look at "The Thinker", scanning their eyes from the base of the statue, slowly, all the way up to his pensive head, resting upon his tightly clenched fist. At that moment, the entire party half expected the statue to break its present pose and reach down and grab them all. Thankfully, that didn't happen. Instead, each teen scooted quickly around the pedestal and ran for the front doors as fast as they could. "The Thinker" never altered his expression, remaining forward-focused in his deep study of the boulevard that stretched out in front of his stone perch.

As the group gathered at the front desk, they were met by a

friendly docent who seemed to know who they were and what their purpose was for being there.

"Are you children here for Dr. Beele?" she asked with a reassuring, welcoming tone.

Tom answered for the group, "Yes we are. I called ahead to let him know that we'd be visiting."

The docent smiled and handed them each a visitor's badge. "You can go right up, dears. Take the private elevator, he's already expecting you."

With that, AJ, Vic and Lynni followed Tom and Elly as they snaked their way down hidden corridors and hallways to the private elevators. When they reached the executive office suite, the doors opened upon the familiar and welcoming office of Dr. Hieronymus S. Beele.

"Well, this is quite an entourage you have brought with you!" Dr. Beele exclaimed as he got up from his mahogany desk. With a glinty grin and a cheerful expression, he greeted each of the teens one by one. The final greetings fell upon Tom and Elly and both of them noticed a slight, disconcerted change in Dr. Beele's face as he shook each of their hands warmly.

After these brief, yet hospitable introductions, the curator guided the teenagers deeper into his office, where a familiar silver tea set had been arranged with six cups and saucers and an assortment of tea cookies and scones. Dr. Beele poured the piping hot Earl Grey tea, while he began his gentle questioning.

"It certainly was a nice surprise to receive your call today. But I am curious as to what brings all of you back into my neck of the woods?"

Without any vote or anyone really talking about it, Tom became the unofficial spokesperson for the group, "Well Doc, "Tom began, "It's like I said on the phone. A lot of weird things have been happening to us lately and now we know why – the Nain Rouge is back!"

No one had gotten used to hearing that statement delivered so bluntly. You could see the rest of the group cringe a little as Tom told the story of eerie feelings, the basketball game, the appearance of Lutin, and then the odd story about the bridge in Washington D. C.

Beele seemed less affected by the news. It was clear that he was listening intently by the way his eyes moved and his brow furrowed as Tom relayed the tales taken from the last few days. When Tom had finished, Dr. Beele moved slowly away from the teens and made his way back to his desk chair. He sat down, still in deep thought and adjusted the computer screen that sat squarely to one side of his massive desk.

Without speaking, Beele typed a few things out on his keyboard and continued to stare, concentrating on the information that was appearing rapidly upon his desktop screen. These few minutes of awkward silence left AJ, Vic and Lynni confused and feeling a bit unsettled. Tom and Elly were used to it. They knew that Dr. Beele was assessing their situation and searching for more information before he would weigh in on the issue at hand.

From behind the computer, the children began to hear broken phrases from the good doctor, "Intriguing… most interesting… and still, quite puzzling…"

"What is going on?" AJ finally broke the uncomfortable spell, "Can you tell us ANYTHING, Dr. Beele?"

The curator peeked out from behind his computer, adjusting his glasses slightly away from the end of his nose, "Well AJ, I won't tell you just anything. But I will tell you something – something quite fascinating."

With that, Dr. Beele waved the children over to computer screen on his desk. He pointed to a small article listed under "Science and Nature" on the national news web site. The children began to read the tiny text that spread across the bottom of the screen,

"…Unusually high water levels have left residents in Midwestern flood plains concerned about increased danger of late winter flooding. In seemingly unrelated news, both the eastern and western coasts of the United States are reporting more frequent storm surges from both the Atlantic and Pacific oceans. Scientists

do not see the rise in water activity related and are still researching various factors that may be causing these activities around the country..."

Elly looked over at Tom from the other side of the desk with a puzzled, almost frustrated expression, "Looks like another puzzle from our doctor friend."

Tom nodded in agreement and stepped back from the desk to face the curator as he sat in his wheeled leather desk chair. "So, what does all this mean, Doc? You seem to know something that you aren't sharing with us."

"Well," Beele began as he pushed himself away from his desk, stood up and walked around to the front of the room; "There seems to be a common theme or thread that is tying all these activities together – water."

"Water?" Lynni piped up, "What does water have to do with the Nain Rouge?"

"Yeah," Vic added, "That doesn't make any sense."

"Well," Beele continued, "It would make sense if you knew that Lutin was a water spirit..."

A sudden, surprised look leaped across the faces of the group. Lynni shot a look at Elly. Elly looked at Vic, Vic locked eyes with Tom, and AJ just stared blankly at the computer screen again.

As the teens struggled for a deeper understanding of Dr.

Beele's words, he made his way over to the wall of ancient books that had revealed other mysteries about the Nain Rouge a few years earlier. The curator rolled his wooden step stool over to one section of the bookshelf and reached up for a single volume, "Westminster's Catalog of Spirits: Volume III - Woodland and Water Creatures".

The group re-gathered in their chairs and on the soft couch as Dr. Beele leafed through the book to find the exact information that he was looking for.

"Ah yes, here it is," he said with quiet satisfaction, "I remember discovering this passage some years ago."

The curator turned toward the teens and began to read a passage, describing Lutin as a water spirit, who, "May draw strength and power from various sources of water, including the ability to manipulate the movement of water, its ebbing, flowing and tidal cycles…"

Beele then flipped over a few more pages. "There is actually a quote in here, attributed to Lutin himself, if you would believe it. This author's convinced that people have heard the dwarf chant,

'Where the water meets land and land meets the sea,
Between shadow and sun is where I shall be.'

Elly looked over at Tom, "That sounds like something Lutin

would say…"

"That may be our explanation for the sudden increase in water-related incidents around the country; for the bridge in Washington D. C." Dr. Beele concluded as he closed the book and returned it to its rightful place on the massive shelf, "Now that he is free, he could be getting more powerful in areas where the land meets the water."

Elly was the first to speak, "I think that you're on to something. Remember, Lutin was the 'Keeper of the Straits', he protected the water and the land around Detroit until Cadillac and his men shunned him and brought the curse to the city."

"That's right," Tom added, "Now that he's free, maybe he can draw from the water and land as an energy source, making more trouble for everybody."

Things were starting to make a bit more sense now. Vic, AJ and Lynni were beginning to see how much trouble Elly and Tom had been in when they fought Lutin the first time. The realization that they too were being sucked into the vortex of his power was now becoming apparent to them.

"What I still don't understand," AJ asked after a brief moment, "Is how did the Nain Rouge get to Washington D.C . from Royal Oak so quickly? I mean, it's not like he can fly… can he?"

"That is a valid, yet puzzling question," Dr. Beele responded. "To my knowledge, Lutin cannot fly, glide or even propel himself great distances. His ability to appear and disappear at will seems to be more of an illusion than any tangible, actual imbued power or talent. These facts, along with Lutin's unexplained targets for trouble, serve only as added pieces to our ever-expanding puzzle."

Why had Lutin broken up a high school basketball game in Michigan and then attacked a bridge outside of Washington D.C. on the same night?

The curator returned to his tea service, refreshing everyone's cup with some more hot tea. The group sat quietly, mulling over the discoveries that had been made in their brief meeting with Dr. Beele.

Hieronymus sat across from the teens, rubbing his chin between his thumb and forefinger, as if this gentle motion might release some stuck thought or an undiscovered idea that may have become lodged in that complex brain of his.

But it was no use. As the sun began sinking over the Detroit Historical Museum across the street, no one could come up with any more ideas regarding Lutin's return or his motivation for disaster and destruction. Worse yet, neither Dr. Beele nor the teenagers had any idea as to where the Nain Rouge might strike next.

As the afternoon subtly slipped into evening, the entire entourage sat in quiet seclusion, silently agreeing that as so many thoughts ran through their heads, it was the not knowing that was the scariest thought of all.

Chapter 9
The Not Knowing

Splashed *across the* morning paper was the headline:

"Double Trouble: Natural Disasters Hit San Francisco"

Vic came down for breakfast and saw the front page of the

paper flutter softly between his dad's hands as he sat at the breakfast table, enjoying his morning coffee. Vic grabbed his dad's hands to hold the newspaper still, as he read the news article, still floating in front of his dad's face:

"...San Francisco was rocked last night by 6.3 magnitude earthquake, accompanied by scattered flooding throughout regions of Northern California. Damage assessments have yet to be officially released, but early reports by local news agencies indicate severe damage to urban areas, major buildings and transportation systems..."

Vic dropped down onto his kitchen chair like a 50 lbs. bag of Idaho potatoes. In any other situation, he would have not even noticed the grim front page headlines. Like most teenagers, Vic was usually more concerned with homework, girls and hanging out with his friends. A natural disaster half way across the country would not normally get his attention, especially first thing in the morning. But now things were different. For some reason, Vic knew that the headline was linked to the Nain Rouge.

The worst news was that his sister was out there. His older sister, Rachel had just moved out there last fall for college. She was attending Santa Clara University in the San Francisco Bay area.

"What about Rachel, is she OK?" Vic asked his dad, who

finally set down the paper, revealing the deep concern on his face.

"She's OK Vic," his father reassured him. "We were able to get a hold of her last night, once we heard the reports on the late night news. Her dorms were damaged a little, but the campus took less of a hit than the city center. She's fine now and she's safe, that's what matters most."

Vic felt a little better, but not much. He really needed to talk to his friends. Maybe that would help slow the racing thoughts that were whizzing around his head.

It was not until the afternoon that all of the teens had a chance to re-connect. After the last bell from the end of 6th hour rang, Tom, Elly, Vic AJ and Lynni met in the courtyard with a few hundred other students, waiting for their rides home from school.

"Did you guys hear about San Francisco?" Vic began.

The group looked back at Vic with a mixed bag of faces. Some faces looked serious and knowing. Others looked confused and concerned.

"What did you hear?" Elly asked in a low whisper.

"It was on the web," Vic answered, "Flooding and earthquakes mostly... sounds like the work of Lutin to me..."

Tom became suddenly aware of the dozens of people around them. He took out a notebook and opened it up, creating a distraction that would draw his friends into a tighter circle, while allowing for the other outsiders to move away with disinterest.

"Ok guys," Tom spoke quietly, "These could be just natural occurrences. But I'm beginning to doubt that. Things are just happening too frequently now, all over the map. We have got to find out what the Nain Rouge is up to… and fast."

"What's your hurry?" came a slithery, raspy voice that seemed to emanate from the backs of the teenagers throats, "You youngsters are always in such a hurry to figure things out – never take any time to just slow down to stop and smell the roses…".

The tight circle broke into five large pieces as the group jumped back away from each other. Each child looked at the other, thinking that the ominous, intimidating words had come out of someone else's mouth like some sort of ventriloquist under demonic possession.

In their panic, AJ had turned around and noticed a little man sitting casually with one leg crossed over the other on one of the courtyard benches.

"Look!" AJ directed the group's attention over to the occupied bench.

"Lutin!" Vic yelled and without warning, dove at the creature that sat so serene and self-assured just a few feet away. Vic smashed his elbows on the braided steel bench and came up with nothing in hands but some foul-smelling air and a little smoke.

Lutin stood behind the boy, clicking his tongue in mock shame and disgust. "Now now, is that any way to treat a guest? And, what did you think you were going to do if you caught me, stupid boy? I am free and unfettered now, like wind through the trees... whether fallen or upright..."

With that statement, Lutin grinned with evil delight, looking over in the general direction where the great Oak had fallen and almost killed the teens only a few nights earlier.

Tom came over and helped Vic up off of the ground.

"What do you want with us?" Tom spoke plainly and forcefully to the Nain Rouge.

"I am not at liberty to discuss that with you, Thomas," Lutin replied coolly, "I have realized the error of my ways in sharing too much information with you in the past. No, what I want from you and your friends, you are already giving to me. So, please continue with your conjecture and puzzling...".

With those words, Lutin smiled a wicked smile and evaporated into the air with his fiendish feline grin smeared like grease paint across his face.

Everyone in the group looked around the courtyard to see if anyone had noticed the commotion. Strangely enough, no one had. Everyone appeared to be talking, walking and moving about as if nothing abnormal had happened - like an evil dwarf popping up out of nowhere, heckling and tormenting a small group of teenagers.

Lynni looked more worried than ever, "Guys, this is really bad.

I don't like what's happening to us – it is like things are getting worse and weirder all the time."

"Well, I don't know about things getting worse," Tom interjected, "But they sure are getting weirder… It's obvious that Lutin is enjoying playing with our heads. He wants us to know that he is up to something, but he doesn't want us to know exactly what it is".

"Tom's right," Elly added, "We defeated him last time because he made the mistake of revealing too much. I know he'll never make that mistake again. We are going to have to figure this out for ourselves."

"Yeah, and we better hurry up. I think Lutin's troublemaking has just begun," AJ piped in. "I think that Washington and San Francisco are just the start."

With that heavy thought, the weight of silence fell over the teenagers as they sat in the courtyard trying to figure out what to do next. It was as if they were trying to sort out a thousand-piece jigsaw puzzle without any picture on the box. In reality, they had very little idea as to what the mystery was that they were trying to solve.

As the friends made their way down Crooks Road toward their respective subdivisions, they continued to talk and conjecture as to what the possibilities of Lutin's return could be. Just as they were passing Oakridge Market, the troupe stopped at the traffic light where Crooks Road met Webster Road. This was the spot that the friends usually disbursed, making their individual ways down other side streets to their own houses.

It was at this point, just before everyone began their goodbyes and see-ya-laters, that AJ got a wild, almost wonderful look in eyes.

"What is it AJ?" Vic said as he grabbed AJ by his upper arm.

"I think I've got it," AJ replied in a sort of a dreamy, far-off tone.

"What've you got?" the group seemed to ask in unison.

"Part of the puzzle…" was AJ's vague response, "I don't really know why the Nain Rouge is doing what he's doing, but I might know how he's doing it."

"Really, how?!!" said the group again, each at a different time but all within a few seconds of each other.

"Let's go back to my house and I'll show you," said AJ as he looked more and more sure of himself.

So they did. AJ led Tom, Elly, Vic and Lynni back to his house, refusing to acknowledge any more of their persistent questioning until he could show them what he had to show them.

Chapter 10
Underground

*A**J's backyard stretched** behind his tri-level house for an extra two lots. When the architects designed his subdivision after World War II, they skipped one thru street on the planning grid, giving his block deeper backyards than the rest of the neighborhood.

His house was located near the corner of Main Street and Vinsetta Boulevard. The boulevard had once been part of the southeastern Michigan watershed that flowed into Lake St. Clair. Before the 1930's, the boulevard had actually been a river called the Red Run. As the city grew, new homes were designed for the valley around the Red Run. Since the area tended to flood quite often in the spring, city planners diverted the river with a giant drainage pipe. They then covered the river and pipe with dirt, grass and shrubs to create the boulevard that now separated the two sides of AJ's street. It was now a ghost river; still running and flowing underneath the ground, yet quiet and invisible to the people above.

AJ's dog, Pip, met the teenagers at the backyard fence. AJ led everyone to the far corner of the yard, near some large, looming silver maple trees. This corner of the lot seemed so much darker than the rest of the area. Even though it was mid-afternoon, and there were no leaves on those frozen, ancient trees, it felt much darker, colder and desolate than the rest of the neighborhood.

"Where are you taking us AJ?" Elly questioned from the back of the group.

"Yeah, what gives?" Vic pestered, "Did you want to show off the snowman you built or something?"

AJ was silent as he bent down and wiped the frozen snow away from what looked like a rusted, old manhole cover. As the rest of the group watched, Tom wondered out loud, "What is a sewer cover doing in your backyard AJ?"

Just then, Pip began barking wildly. She sprinted over to where AJ was kneeling and began ducking her white head under his, as if to push him away from the heavy metal cover that rested firmly in the ground.

"Pip!" AJ yelled, "Settle down!" AJ scooped up Pip and shuffled through the melting snow to put her back into the house. As he returned to the corner of the yard, he could see the rest of the teens still standing around the covered hole, silently trying to figure out what could be beneath the ground under their feet.

"Sorry guys," AJ said as he returned to the group, "Pip never likes it when I go back to this part of the yard… Well, anyway, this is it. This is what I wanted to show you."

The group stared at AJ, looking rather underwhelmed.

"So…. what's the big deal?" Vic quipped.

AJ stood to one side of the heavy iron lid, "No one is supposed to know about this… it's a passageway… a passageway down to the ghost river."

The teens all looked at each with a sort of knowing confusion. They all knew that this hole in the ground had something to do with the mystery that they were caught up in, but no real connection had been made yet.

Tom broke the awkward silence, asking, "Why are you

showing this to us AJ? What does it mean?"

AJ crouched down on one knee and tapped the cold metal cover with his index finger, "I think this is how he's been traveling."

"Who has been traveling?" Lynni asked.

"Lutin." AJ responded bluntly. "Ever since I learned that he was a water spirit, I have been thinking about this place. When they covered up the Red Run, they created a few service access points for the water department. This manhole leads directly down to the river that's still running beneath our feet. Lutin could be using these access points to appear and disappear at will.

Not one of the teenagers doubted what AJ was saying. It all seemed quite plausible that the Nain Rouge could be using these portals to move about the city and the region.

"I say we go down and check it out!" Tom exclaimed with a new sense of excitement and anticipation. His renewed energy was met with a mixed reaction of fear, doubt and some lukewarm support for his impetuous plan.

"Are you nuts?" Vic wondered, "You have no idea what's down there or even where that tunnel leads. We could be walking into our own funeral."

"I've been down there before," AJ interjected. "There are some service lights along the passageway, so you can see where you are going for at least a little while. I've never gone too far past the entrance, though. There's a catwalk along the side of the river, so if you're careful, you won't get wet."

"I say we go for it!" Elly stated firmly. "If we all stay together, we should be fine."

The only one who did not weigh in on the plan was Lynni. She just stood there quietly; staring at the iron cover like it was some fascinating work of abstract art. Her eyes seemed to pulse back and forth with an eerie, mesmerizing stare that no one in the group had taken the time to notice. Everyone was too busy to notice Lynni staring intently past the iron cover, as if she were being drawn down into the darkness just beneath the frozen surface where they were standing.

AJ ran back into the house to grab some flashlights, some rope and an emergency medical kit. His dog, Pip, had never stopped barking. She seemed to know what the teens were about to do and her animal instincts were telling her not to let AJ and his friends go down into that dark hole.

By the time AJ returned with the supplies, Tom and Vic had pried the cover off of the manhole with a thick, short branch that had fallen from the maple tree.

"Ok, I've got everything we need," AJ said, a bit out of breath.

"So, who's going to be the first to slide down into the creepy hole?" Vic asked with an over-dramatic, pseudo-scary tone in his voice.

"Cut it out Vic," Elly shot back, "I don't see *you* jumping up to volunteer…"

Elly was right. Everyone was scared to climb down into the shadowy unknown. Vic was just trying to make light of the situation in order to break the tension a little.

After a brief discussion about how to proceed, Tom volunteered to head down the hole first. AJ would then hand down the supplies and the rest of the team would follow. A steel ladder mounted to the side of the entrance made the climb down much easier than Tom expected. It was about a 10-feet drop from the ground to the surface of the tunnel, so Tom was very grateful that the ladder supported his weight so easily.

Once Tom let everyone know that he had made it safely to the bottom, AJ lowered the supplies to him in a bucket tied with a long nylon rope. Tom then used his flashlight to illuminate the entrance while the rest of the group slowly lowered themselves down to where he was waiting.

The last one to remain on the surface was Lynni. She had barely budged since the teens began their journey downward.

"C'mon Lynni!" Elly yelled from below the ground, "It's easy to get down here now."

Lynni finally moved. She got down on her hands and knees on the wet, cold ground. Elly, Tom, Vic and AJ could see her face looking down at them, backlit by the late afternoon sun that hung so weakly in the winter sky.

The children were horrified at what they saw. Suddenly, the face that peered down at them no longer looked like Lynni. Her blue eyes were now a crimson red and her face had been contorted into an evil, menacing grin.

"Fools…" hissed a voice that seemed to come from Lynni's lips but was not her own, "You underestimate me…"

"Lutin!" Tom yelled, "Leave her alone!"

"I am not the one who left her alone, boy, you did," Lutin replied through Lynni's mouth, with sickly sweetness.

With that, the iron cover began to slowly slide back over the hole. All of the teens could hear Lutin cackling and hissing in gleeful delight. Just before the natural light from above was completely snuffed out, they all heard the Nain Rouge whisper through Lynni,

"Oh how lost are the sheep that are ne'er to be found
Left now for dead by the wolf underground…"

Lutin's voice trailed off as Lynni's face disappeared completely. The iron lid shut with a dull, heavy thud, sealing in the darkness that could only be fought off by the pink-white glow from their weakening flashlights.

In that instance, no one said a word, no one breathed and no one knew what would happen next.

Chapter 11
The Ghost River

AJ climbed quickly up the ladder and pushed as hard as he could against the cover. It wouldn't budge, not even an inch.

"Lutin must have blocked it with something. It won't move!" AJ called back down to his friends.

The friends stepped slowly away from the entrance of the tunnel as AJ made his way back down the ladder. As the initial shock from their entrapment wore off, they began to survey their surroundings. Though their vision was limited by the weak beams of their flashlights, they could begin to make out the overall shape of the tunnel, the directional flow of the river and the amount of space they had on the walkway.

"Do you think Lynni is alright?" Elly blurted out with a sense of deep concern.

"I think she'll be fine," Tom answered with quick reassurance. "Lutin only uses what he needs and then discards it. He probably picked Lynni because she was the most scared and vulnerable. The Nain Rouge feeds on fear, remember? He used Lynni to do his dirty work and trap us down here. What use would he have for her now?"

As the teens pondered Lynni's fate, they each noticed that the air in the long chamber had become a warm mix of ozone and sulphury metal that stung their nostrils when they inhaled too deeply. Despite the late winter that froze the ground above their heads, this elongated cavern was not cold at all. In fact, the teens began to sweat a little bit from the humidity of the warm air that circulated above the rushing water.

As they took their winter coats off, Tom was the first to speak, "Guys, I think our best bet is to start walking and look for another way out of this place."

"Yeah," AJ agreed, "I've never walked too far down the tunnel, but I know that it goes on for a long way. There must be another entrance somewhere."

"Well, I say we get going then," Vic interrupted. "I'm tired of standing here waiting for something else bad to happen."

The group quietly agreed and began to make their way down the dark corridor, led only by the dimming yellow glow of their plastic flashlights.

As the teens walked along the dark, foreboding passageway, the only sounds they heard were the gentle whooshing of the Red Run beside them and the infrequent squeaking of unseen water rats that inhabited the forgotten tunnel. It seemed as if hours were passing, as the investigators searched every nook and cranny for another way out.

Time has a way of slowing down in the darkness. Without any point of reference or anything new to look at, it seemed as if the kids were on some sinister steel treadmill, walking and walking and walking without ever really getting anywhere.

"How long are we going to keep walking?" complained Vic, "Let's just turn back before it gets too late!"

"No!" Tom and Elly both said firmly.

Tom added, "We have to just keep moving forward. It only makes sense that there would be another access point somewhere along this passage – there just has to be."

AJ broke into the conversation, "I don't think that is our biggest problem right now, look!"

AJ was right. At the very edge of the flashlight beams, the group could see their singular tunnel splitting up into multiple waterways. Each tributary flowed away from the main tunnel that they were in, pulling the water in both eastern and southern directions.

"Which way do we go now?" AJ questioned.

Tom answered quickly, "Let's keep on our same course, south. This water is flowing right toward Lake St. Clair."

"Tom is probably right," Elly added, "The closer we get to the big lakes, the more likely we are to hit another entryway."

No one disagreed with this logic. The teens followed the same direction they had been traveling all along, moving along a single artery of the river for what seemed like miles.

In the time that passed, little was said between the friends. It was as if the tension and pressure of the day had been slowly building up in the shadowy, confined space that had become their prison. Nobody wanted to acknowledge that they might never see the light of day again. The silence they created in their constant movement forward was a way of denying the inevitable danger that they were in. By simply moving, they were telling each other that there was still hope. No one wanted to break that spell with words of discouragement, fear or panic; even if these were the very things that ran through their thoughts.

Chapter 12
Ley Lines

The flashlight beams were fading. Elly, Tom, Vic and AJ had been walking for hours, maybe even days. No one knew where they were or how far they had traveled. What they did know was that they were exhausted almost to the point of giving in to Lutin's infernal trap.

"Look, over there!" Elly shouted in a weary, raspy voice.

The teens slowly turned their heads over to a corner of the tunnel. There, about five feet above the catwalk they saw it.

"An opening!" Vic shouted with renewed energy.

Vic and AJ charged over to the heavy iron circle that set just above their heads. Vic climbed a service ladder that had been bolted to the side of the passageway.

"I think I can push it up if you help me, AJ" Vic grunted as AJ stepped lightly next to him on the ladder. With the two of them pressing their shoulders up against the heavy cover, it began to move. Tom and Elly watched from below as Vic and AJ carefully lifted the manhole cover up, away from the recessed hole.

In an instant, dull, gray light pierced the darkness of their steel and concrete tomb. The smell of fresh air and asphalt filled the entrance to the cavern as Tom and Elly smiled widely up at Vic and AJ.

"You guys did it!" Tom yelled with excitement and relief.

"We all did it." AJ shouted back down with renewed confidence.

"Yeah," Vic added. "And you're not going to believe where we are."

Tom and Elly looked at each for a brief second and then clambered up the service ladder to the surface. As her head peeked out from the hole first, Elly looked like an inquisitive groundhog, assessing the late winter wind for signs of an early spring. AJ and Vic helped Tom and Elly out of the entrance and onto a grassy area near a familiar street and sidewalk.

"No… way…" Elly gasped as she finally took in all of her surroundings.

"Way…" replied Tom with equal disbelief.

As the scene came into greater focus, the group realized where they were. They had popped out of the ground like four, worn winter daisies – right behind the Detroit Institute of Arts!

It was night time and the stars shined bright in the late winter sky. The DIA cast a shadow on the children as they looked across John R Street at the Center for Creative Studies and down the block at the Detroit Science Center, which led further into the center of the city.

"Who would have thought that we'd end up here?" Tom wondered.

"I guess it makes sense," AJ replied, "I mean, we know that Lutin has been seen where we came in and where we came out of the tunnel, right?"

"That means that he has been using these tunnels to appear and disappear for sure!" Vic concluded.

"You're partially right," Elly added. "There is more to the story than just that. And I know who could fill in the details for us."

With that, the boys watched as Elly pointed skyward to one of the upper floors of the DIA. A light was on in a third floor window. "Dr. Beele is still in his office working. Let's see what he has to say about all of this."

The teens moved quickly through the chilly night air, leaving a smoky trail of hot breath that mingled with the sewer steam that rose up from the iron grates in the street. As they reached a service entrance at the back of the DIA Administration Building, they jumped back a little in surprise. Already in the doorway was a familiar, shadowy figure, gently pushing the door open for them.

"Good evening, my friends," the shadow said softly. 'I saw you in the street from my office window. I assumed that you were coming to see me."

"Dr. Beele?" Tom asked, still slightly startled.

"Who else would you expect at such a late hour?" Dr. Beele quipped as he stepped into the light, "The Nain Rouge, perhaps?"

"Not funny, Doc." Vic shot back, "If you knew what we've been through, you'd see how NOT funny that really is."

"I apologize for my attempt at levity," the curator said with genuine contrition, "I meant nothing by it and I can see by your faces and your clothes that you have been through much tonight. Come then, let's go up to my office and you can tell me all that you need to tell me."

In a matter of minutes, the entire crew was warmly wrapped up around the fireplace in Dr. Beele's office, sipping China Black tea and nibbling on the best tea cakes and scones in the city.

The young gatherers were so fatigued from their journey that it seemed no one had the energy to speak. Finally, Elly mumbled a quiet question directed at the pensive curator,

"Dr. Beele, do you know what's going on?"

"Perhaps," was his equally quiet, but thoughtful response.

"It seems to me that you have inadvertently discovered ley lines."

AJ and Vic questioned in unison, "Ley lines?"

"Yes," Beele responded with little emotion, "ley lines. There are some people that believe that there are lines of actual psychic, electromagnetic energy running through the earth. Many sacred, significant buildings and monuments around the globe have been built at the points where these ley lines intersect, points of powerful energy. Stonehenge, the Cathedral of Notre Dame, the Taj Mahal, the Washington Monument are just a few examples of the places where these ley lines are purported to intersect. Ironically, even this museum has been rumored to have been built above an intersection of ley lines."

"Unbelievable!" Tom blurted out. "Do you mean to tell me that Lutin has been riding some sort of psychic highway underground, causing trouble wherever he wants?"

"It would not surprise me in the least, given the fact that you have found his secret passageway. It would seem quite logical that the sewer systems were built along ancient ley lines. As the water flows, so does the natural energy that is all around us. If this is true, with the curse broken, the Nain Rouge is now empowered to travel along his 'psychic highway', as you so colorfully put it, as he so chooses."

It was after this statement that Dr. Beele's face finally began to show some emotion and concern. It was as if his assessment of the situation was just becoming as real to himself as it was for the teenagers. He was beginning to acknowledge that the ultimate intent of the Nain Rouge was far more real and dangerous than even he had imagined.

The room had grown very still and quiet. No one was willing to look at anyone else, for fear of what they might see in each other's eyes.

For now, they all knew, for sure, that the Nain Rouge was back and free to roam anywhere he wanted. It was as if they all heard the distant horn of an oncoming freight train, growing closer and more powerful in the distance. As they sat in the comfort of the curator's office, no one wanted to admit that the train was bearing down upon them and there was nothing they could do to stop it.

Chapter 13
Water, Water, Everywhere

L*ynni woke up* on the cold, snowy ground as moonlight tried to pierce through the heavy, gray clouds that had gathered once again in the February sky.

"Lynni!" voices joined in unison and called out in the distance.

She wanted to respond but was still too dizzy to even stand up. In less than a moment, she was surrounded by Tom, Elly Vic, AJ and Dr. Beele.

"What just happened? Where am I?" Lynni babbled incoherently.

Dr. Beele did not bother to respond to her ramblings and instead, instructed the children to get her back into AJ's house to warm her up. With very little effort, the group gathered up the flopping legs and arms of their friend and brought her into the house.

Once Lynni was sufficiently wrapped up in a few colorful quilts and AJ's favorite blue Snuggie, (with a cup of hot chocolate to bring her back to life), the teens felt better about asking her some questions.

"Lynni, what do you remember about the past few hours?" Tom asked her calmly.

"Well," Lynni responded in a quiet, slow whisper, "The last thing I remember was staring down the manhole at you guys. I was thinking about how I really didn't want to go down there. I was hoping that you guys would come back up and we could just forget the whole thing. Then it happened…"

"What happened?" Vic asked anxiously.

"Well, I'm not really sure," Lynni continued, "I was just about to take my first step toward the ladder, when a voice began to hiss inside my head. It kept mumbling something about a wolf stealing sheep, or something like that."

Lynni shuddered and grew strangely quiet again. The teens watched as the images that ran through her head were displayed in the furrows and frowns that now danced across her face.

"Lynni, what is it?" Elly gently shook Lynni by the shoulder, as if to bring her out of a terrible trance.

"That voice… that voice" Lynni repeated in a hushed whisper. "The voice grew louder in my head, I couldn't stop it. It was like it was taking me over – first my head, then my heart, then the rest of my body. That voice – it was like a cold, damp net that was thrown over me – dragging through me – trapping me, taking me over…I'm sorry you guys… I'm so sorry…"

"It was Lutin, my dear." Hieronymus Beele's voice broke the tension that had been building within Lynni's revelation. "It was Lutin who did these things, not you. You are a victim of his evil, not the perpetrator."

The rest of the teens gathered around Lynni, reassuring her that everything would be alright and that she wasn't to blame for anything. Lutin was the cause of all this trouble and he now had resorted to possession to force his will upon others.

The curator pulled Tom and Elly aside, as the others continued to console Lynni. "Tonight has been very illuminating on many fronts." The doctor spoke discreetly. "Lutin is clearly working toward some sort of master plan, of which I fear is bigger than the personal revenge he pursued in the past. I still have more questions to be answered before I can say for sure. There are a few matters I have to take care of out of town, specifically related to this matter. Unfortunately, these activities will separate us for a few weeks. That is why I need you two to help me."

"Sure Doc, anything you need," was Tom's quick reply. Elly looked at Tom and Dr. Beele and nodded vigorously.

"Excellent, I need you both keep an eye on things while I am away. On the 19th of March, I will require your presence in my offices at the DIA at precisely three o'clock. I should have much more to share with you at that time."

Tom and Elly looked at each other, a bit puzzled and slightly nervous at Dr. Beele's request.

"What's going on, Dr. Beele? Where are you going?" Tom asked directly.

"Tom, Elly," "Hieronymus began in quiet seriousness, " The events of these past few days have solidified for me the grave nature of Lutin's intent. Where I am going is less important than what I have to do. I will reveal all upon my return, I promise."

"When will you be back?" Elly asked.

"It should not be more than a few weeks, by the 19th of March for certain" Beele replied matter-of-factly.

With that, the curator gave them both a reassuring smile and returned back to the group.

The doctor spoke firmly, with great clarity to the teens, "I am glad we are all safe and sound. Now you all should go home and get some sleep. We can sort this matter out when we have all had some rest and have given ourselves sufficient time to clear our heads. I am confident that we will all be busy sorting this mess out for weeks to come. We all must work together, for I fear that the water is rising around us more quickly than we think."

Chapter 14
Small Hopes

In the weeks to come it was all over the news; increased flooding in the Mid-Atlantic and Plains States, property damage throughout the country and people left homeless. Tom, Elly, Vic, AJ and Lynni felt helpless as they trudged through the late winter and into spring. Dr. Beele was nowhere to be found

It was finally Friday and the kids could not wait to unplug their brains for the weekend. No one had any specific plans. They agreed that just hanging out, watching movies and playing video games was probably the best and safest way to numb their skulls and forget about their situation until Dr. Beele's return.

Friday night found the group right where they wanted to be, down in AJ's basement, playing his 3-D Pomuchi Game. In five-player mode, the teens traveled through a fantasy role-playing world, where each player was imbued with certain powers and abilities to help them on their quest. Tom was a white-fanged battle beast, Elly a stealthy ninja, Vic a nomadic warrior, Lynni an emerald enchantress, and AJ a crafty archer. The team traveled together, down dark roads and through forbidden forests in search of the twelve stones of Ularga.

"Hey, does it seem like it is getting darker in here?" AJ asked, looking away from the TV screen.

"We're in an enchanted forest, you dink, it's supposed to be dark," Vic spat out these words as his eyes never left the action on the screen.

"No," AJ insisted, out here, not in there. It is darker than it was..."

Just then, in the middle of their battle, came an odd character onto to the video screen. It looked like some sort of dark dwarf. The only difference was that this figure pulsated with clarity and dimension. There was no fuzziness or pixilation about this image. It danced, jumped and hopped around just like...

AJ 's dog Pip began to bark and howl at the T.V. as if in great alarm and pain.

"N-Nain Rouge!" Lynni screamed.

It was right at that moment that all five game controllers glowed red and intense like burning embers. The group dropped the burning controllers, shouting in surprise and pain.

"Hello fellow travelers, and welcome to my humble wood," came a familiar, slimy voice from the Pomuchi Game.

No one knew what to say. Vic was inclined to put his foot right through the TV screen, but he was still too stunned to do anything at all.

"I don't want to keep you from your fun," Lutin chided them with mock sincerity," I just wanted to check up on my favorite children to see how they were faring."

AJ was about to say something, but Elly grabbed his arm and looked at him with a stern eye. Dr. Beele had warned before he left that Lutin might return, seeking information about how much they knew about his plans. The curator cautioned the teens that Lutin would taunt them, goad them into revealing anything they might know about all of his evil activities.

So, instead of yelling at the Nain Rouge or trying to capture or secure him, they simply sat there in stunned silence, repressing any urges to attack or take flight.

"What's the matter little ones, cat got your tongue?" Lutin egged them on but to no avail. The teens just continued to sit there, staring at him upon the screen.

"Nothing to say? Well that's just fine! Keep your mouths shut for an eternity for all I care. You see, my power grows. It grows every minute of every day. With each bridge I knock down, with each river or lake I swell to flooding, it grows! I am becoming all-powerful and there is nothing you can do about it! It's just fine, just fine with me if you want to watch silently as I tear your little world apart. It will all be mine soon – rightfully mine!"

With those final words, there was a bright flash from the video screen. The little red dwarf shot a bolt of lightning from his fingers and blew up the warrior, the archer, the enchantress, the ninja and the battle beast within the game. Their characters were destroyed. A loud electrical POP came from the television and then complete darkness. Lutin was gone and all that remained was the faint whiff of ozone and a lingering charge of static electricity in the air.

AJ was the first to move. He groped his way along the floor and wall to the circuit box. He flipped a number of circuit breakers until he found the right one and the basement lights came back on.

As the light returned, the teens slowly began to break free from the trance that had held them so tightly only minutes before.

"Is everyone OK?" Elly asked out loud as she looked around

the room.

"Yeah, we're all fine, I think," Vic responded in a slow, stupefied tone.

AJ's dog Pip went around the room with quiet, happy concern, sniffing the feet and licking the faces of the five friends. This small act from such a small dog had a powerful recuperative effect on the entire group. Soon, they were all chatting and discussing the meaning of Lutin's latest visit.

"I wish Dr. Beele was back," Lynni said with a twinge of sadness in her voice.

"I think we all do," Elly responded with reassurance.

"Well, what are we supposed to do now?" Vic piped in with aggravated frustration, "I don't think there's any way to stop Lutin."

Tom sat in the corner of the couch thinking quietly to himself and mumbling, "Power corrupts and absolute power corrupts absolutely…"

"What are you babbling about Tom?" Vic questioned.

"I said, 'Power tends to corrupt and absolute power corrupts absolutely.' Dr. Beele told me that a long time ago. He was quoting Lord Acton, a 19th Century British historian."

"So, what is it supposed to mean?" Lynni wondered.

"I think I get it," AJ jumped in, "Maybe, it means that Lutin thinks he's all-powerful now since he's free from his curse. He can't be stopped, right, Tom?"

"You're kinda right," Tom noted thoughtfully. "Lutin is free from his curse, which does make him more powerful. However, the fact that he believes in his absolute power means that his mind is completely corrupted."

"So where does that leave us?" Lynni asked again.

"It doesn't leave us anywhere," Tom answered. "What it *does* do is give us hope. If Lutin feels his power is absolute, he is completely corrupted and overconfident. He thinks he can't be defeated. His twisted mind may blind him to the good we can do. That means he has a blind spot, a spot where hope can hide until it turns into action."

"I wish Dr. Beele was back," Lynni repeated.

"We all do," Elly said with renewed assurance. "And maybe when he gets back, we can turn our tiny hopes into actions."

Chapter 15
Beele's Return

***I**t had been* over three weeks since Dr. Beele's departure to places unknown. Spring had come to southeastern Michigan, pushing away the cold and the clouds to make way for an unfamiliar sun that had returned to the eastern sky.

While the doctor was away, Elly, Tom, AJ, Vic and Lynni did

their best to get through their classes, homework and the mundane routine of freshman life. Multiple natural disasters were being recorded all over the country. People from different regions were reporting sightings of an odd little creature near some of the disaster sights.

The return of Hieronymus Beele became the only beacon of hope for the confused and frustrated teenagers. They all knew that there was nobody else that they could confide in. No one would believe them, as most of the sightings and disasters were being attributed to natural causes or freak twists of nature. People were writing Lutin's presence off as hearsay or as a figment of the active imaginations of local attention seekers.

As far as the group was concerned, Tom, Elly, AJ, Vic and Lynni were bonded together with one giant secret. It was a secret that no one wanted to keep. But it was a secret that could not be revealed, since no one else would accept it as the truth. The truth that evil was spreading throughout the land, bit by bit, little by little. The Nain Rouge was gaining strength right under everyones' noses.

Elly's phone rang after school, right at 4:00pm. It was Dr. Beele. He was home, he was finally home. Elly felt so much better just hearing his voice. The knot that had been tensing in her stomach for weeks finally began to release its hold.

The curator gave her the following instructions, "Meet me in my offices after school on Friday, just Tom and yourself." His message was brief and to the point and made her feel better with its stark directness.

As soon as Elly got off of the phone with Dr. Beele, she called Tom and let him know the news.

"That's great El, but why just the two of us?" Tom wondered from the other end of the receiver.

"I don't know, but he seemed quite specific in his request." Elly answered, equally puzzled.

"Well, I don't think the others are going to like it one bit," Tom continued, "I mean, we're all in this together, right?"

"You're right Tommy," Elly said, "But I'm just telling you what Dr. Beele told me, that's all."

Tom was right. At lunch the next day, Elly passed the news on to the rest of group. No one could believe it.

"What's the deal?" Vic asked indignantly. "I thought that we were all in this together?"

"That's just what I said when I heard!" Tom added.

Everyone else nodded in agreement with Vic. After everything that they had been through, it seemed like a slap in the face to have only Tom and Elly invited back to the curator's office. With arms folded and brows furrowed, the group stared back and forth at Elly and Tom to see how the two would respond to their disappointment and anger.

Tom looked at Elly for a brief moment before he spoke. "Guys, I don't care what Beele said about us coming alone. We're all going to be there. He doesn't know the half of what we have been through – first Elly and me and then you guys… we stand together, no matter what."

Elly quietly added, "Tommy is right, we all go or nobody goes."

After that, the mood of the group changed for the better. Vic, AJ and Lynni seemed satisfied that Tom and Elly were being supportive, regardless of Dr. Beele's instructions. After all, they had agreed from the very start that no matter what happened, they would all stick together. They had made a pact and it was good to see that Tom and Elly were not willing to break it.

As far as Hieronymus Beele was concerned, he would just have to deal with them directly– all of them.

Chapter 16
Cartography

F_riday finally came_ and dragged its long feet through the slow morning, creeping into the greatly anticipated afternoon. The teens boarded the downtown bus and headed directly down Woodward to the DIA offices.

No one paid much attention as they passed previous points of interest, including the very spot where final conflict with Lutin occurred – at least the spot that where the final conflict was thought to have taken place.

The young ones entered the DIA through the impressive arches of the front entrance. Vic swung open the polished brass doors with the same familiarity of sliding through the side door of AJ's house on his way to the teens' basement hangout.

The security guard stopped them, looking a bit surprised.

"Hey gang, hold up there!" she called to the group. "You are here to see Dr. Beele, right?"

The group nodded in unison.

"Well, I only have clearance for two of you on my security list… Hold on and let me call up to the doctor."

Tom looked over at Vic, who looked over and AJ and Lynni, who were looking at Elly. They were all thinking the same thing, "Maybe we made a mistake."

But it was too late. The security guard was already on the phone to Beele, explaining the situation to him. Her call was brief and before they knew it, they were all being waved over into the staff elevators, heading directly up to the offices of the curator.

Hieronymus Beele met Elly and Tom, blocking his broad doorway with his slender frame and a look that could melt metal.

"Could I have a word with you two, for just a moment?" Beele uttered with deep restraint through his clenched teeth.

Tom gulped and Elly instinctively grabbed his right hand as the two made their way into a side room behind the curator. The rest of the crew filed into Dr. Beele's office and waited quietly, straining to hear what was going on behind those thick, mahogany doors.

"What in the world were you thinking?!!" Beele unleashed an anger that Tom and Elly had never seen before. "I gave you strict instructions to come alone. Now you have dragged your friends along with you. Do you realize the mess we are all in now?"

"Dr. Beele," Elly replied calmly, "We know what you asked, but we're all in this together. We promised AJ, Vic and Lynni that no matter what happened, we would stick together…"

Tom added with a bit more fire in his voice, "You're the one who disappeared for a month and left us hanging - We had to stick it out alone. Now you want to break us up? Forget it, Doc."

Dr. Beele stepped away from Tom and Elly, creating a less confrontational atmosphere. With a bit more distance between them, he turned his back to the teens, his face much warmer than before but with a look of great concern.

"I'm sorry. Truly, I was only looking out for everyone's welfare. What I have discovered, what I now know… I just didn't want anyone else getting hurt. But you are right, both of you. We are all in this together. I was foolish to think otherwise… No more of this now, let's return to the others. It is rude to keep them waiting. Besides, I have much to tell you about my journey; a very interesting journey, indeed."

The curator led Tom and Elly back to his offices where the others were waiting. AJ, Vic and Lynni looked curiously at the trio, trying to gage the content and results of their recent conversation through the expressions on their faces.

"Friends," Dr. Beele said warmly, "I made an error in judgment by not inviting all of you to our meeting today. I am sorry and I hope that you will forgive me for my thick-headedness. It was pointed out to me just this afternoon that we are a team. I never really looked at the situation that way before. Until now - Now I know how true that statement is."

"Don't worry, Doc, we forgive you." Vic said plainly.

"Yeah, all for one and one for all, right guys?" AJ added.

"We're glad to be here, to help any way we can" Lynni concluded.

Everyone nodded in agreement and Dr. Beele continued, "Well then, I am glad that we have settled this affair. Let's not waste a minute more. I have everything ready in the conference room. This way, please."

The curator slid open the heavy, paneled pocket doors leading into his large conference room. In this impressive room, the teens' eyes panned up to see the great crystal chandelier that hung high above the giant oak conference table, balanced in the middle of the room. Beautifully carved cabinets and cupboards ran along either side of the massive table, creating a cathedral effect of height, depth and breadth within this long, narrow room.

Upon the oak table lay a multitude of maps, legends and atlases. The southern wall was completely covered with an oversized map of North America. The map was unlike any other map they had ever seen. From a distance, it appeared to be just an ordinary (albeit very large) topographical map. But as you moved in for a closer look, you could see much greater detail come into focus. It seemed almost magical and surreal how one step forward or one step back could change the focus and detail of the great map.

On it was every state, every city, every town, every lake, river and stream in full color and topography. The detailed representations of the places on the map were uncanny. It was as if someone had taken a satellite picture from space, exploded the view onto the wall and then drawn all of the states, regions cities and streets in minute detail.

Even more striking were the large red push pins that had been driven into various points on the map. A silver thread had been strung between many of the red push pins, creating an intricate web of crisscrossed lines that shimmered in the chandelier light. It was like some oversized arachnid had snuck into the room and spun a web; creating a new, delicate trap for the unsuspecting youths. Everyone wanted to reach out and touch it, but refrained, for fear that they would become hopelessly entwined in the points of intersection.

"What the heck is all this, Doc?" Vic asked.

"They are maps." Beele said with droll discretion.

"We know what maps are," Lynni added a bit indignantly, "But what are all of those pins and lines and string about?"

"Allow me to demonstrate," Beele answered. "AJ, come here and assist me, if you would, please."

The curator handed AJ a large box of red push pins and a short spool of silver thread.

"AJ, I will call out points on the map. As I do, I would like you to place a pin at each point."

"Sure Dr. Beele, no problem." AJ answered with ready determination.

The curator picked up a few sheets of paper and begin to read aloud slowly and clearly:

"Bangor, Maine – the Cole Land Transportation Museum. Scranton Pennsylvania - the Everhart Museum near the Lackawanna River. Yuma, Arizona – the Cocopah Tribal Museum near the Gila River. Las Vegas, Nevada – the Atomic Testing Museum near Lake Mead…"

The list went on and on as Dr. Beele rattled off the names of more cities, more museums and more bodies of water. Eventually,

the rest of the teens grew curious and began peering over the curator's shoulder. Over the top of his shoulder, they saw a chart that contained various cities and states that were associated with specific museums and regional bodies of water. All of these locations were broken up into specific regions around the country:
- Northeast
- Mid-Atlantic
- South
- Southwest
- Midwest.

Beele seemed to ignore their interest as he continued to dictate more locations to AJ with a bit more rhythm and velocity,

"Syracuse, New York – the Erie Canal Museum near Onondaga Lake, Lake Charles, Louisiana – the Calcasieu Museum near Lake Charles, Appleton, Wisconsin – the Outagamie Museum near Green Bay, Redding California – the Schreder Planetarium near the Sacramento River, Wilmington, North Carolina – The Museum of Aviation near Cape Fear…"

Nobody said a word as Dr Beele went through his entire chart, calling out all of his points of interest. The locations on the map magically rose to meet AJ's pushpins. He feverishly placed the red push pins into the appropriate locations on the map, while stringing all of them together with long lines of silver thread.

After what seemed like an entire evening had passed, Lynni

broke the spell by being the first to speak up, "Uh, Dr. Beele, are you going to tell us what this all means? What are all of these places and points and threads supposed to mean?"

As if being lifted from a trance, Beele set down his papers and gently shifted his spectacles down, onto the end of his thin, narrow nose, "Quite right, Lynni, quite right. I'm afraid I was drawn too deeply into my work again."

The museum curator then drew back from the great map and beckoned the rest of the group to do the same. As they all stepped a few feet away from the cartographical masterpiece, they were again awestruck by the intricate web that had been spun during Beele's and AJ's feverish activities.

"So, what is this we are looking at Doc?" Vic piped in as he stared at the massive web covering the giant map.

"What you are seeing ladies and gentlemen, is a grid."

"A grid?", Elly asked slightly confused. "What kind of a grid Dr. Beele?"

"The Red Tide Grid, to be exact, Elly" the curator replied, preparing himself to reveal even more than the teens were expecting.

"When I left all of you a few weeks ago, I had a hunch, an idea, a hypothesis, if you will. I conjectured that the disasters caused by the Nain Rouge all had something in common. The common threads, in this case, silver ones, were water and places of historical significance."

Tom interrupted, "Dr. Beele, we knew that Lutin drew his power and energy from water. We also knew he was drawn to the negative energy of certain places, where he could become even more powerful and cause more trouble. We even figured out how he was traveling, using the ley lines. We just never knew why he was doing all of these things."

"Precisely Tom, that was why I had to leave." Beele continued, "After all of you appeared that evening from the sewers, I postulated that our DIA may be a part of this evil equation. So, in my absence, I traveled to areas where I knew Lutin had been. Sure enough, in every spot, there was a museum nearby. Being a curator with many years of experience to my name, I know quite a few other curators around the country. My network of friends and associates allowed me to confirm what I had suspected for weeks now."

The curator paused to catch his breath and settle his nerves a little. It was becoming quite clear that the grid on the map in long, narrow conference was a display of epic, evil proportion. The entire group hung on Dr. Beele's every word and waited anxiously for him to finally reveal the rest of his discoveries.

After a small sip of water from a crystal pitcher and a few more deep breaths, the curator was ready to continue. "As I was saying, my suspicions were confirmed upon the conclusion of my journey.

The museum sites on this map are points of intersection on the ley line system. Lutin has been using these museums as portals to enter and exit waterways all around the country."

"But why would he use museums, Dr. Beele?" AJ asked, as if in deep thought.

"A valid question, AJ," Beele replied, "Museums are centers of culture and learning and contain various objects and artifacts. These objects often hold energy, left over from their places of origin. This energy can be either good or bad. Great works inspired by love, bravery and concern for humanity generate positive energy. Conversely, objects of war, torture and human strife often carry negative energy. Lutin can use any of this negative energy to add to his power."

"How can a couple of rocks and some statues help him?" Vic chimed in.

"Another fine question," Beele responded, "But it is more than just the artifacts. It is the very location, the very spot on which these museums are built. Many of these museums are built at the intersection of the ley lines, which creates powerful energy for those that know how to use it."

Elly walked over to the wall on which the map hung. She began to traces her fingers along the silver threads that criss-crossed over various regions, states, cities and towns all over the country. "It is a grid... a grid of negative energy."

"Precisely," the curator acknowledged with a voice so quiet and tentative that the rest of the group could hardly hear him say it. "It is the Red Tide Grid. The newspapers and television stations have been reporting on the disasters, but very few have even mentioned the strange discoloration of the water in these regions."

"What is the Red Tide?" Lynni questioned from the back of the room.

"Under normal circumstances, red tides occur when algae blooms and increases rapidly in an aquatic system. In can happen in the ocean or even in freshwater. It is a natural occurrence that may damage the environment and even kill many living creatures in the water."

"But these are not normal circumstances," Tom reminded Dr. Beele.

"Indeed," the curator replied. "It seems a Red Tide has been associated with all of the other natural disasters that have been occurring. Until now, I was the only one who had put the puzzle pieces together and seen the larger picture."

"But what about the grid, Doc?" Vic insisted, "What does the Red Tide have to do with the grid?"

"The grid is the vehicle that allows Lutin's evil to grow. He is playing a game of connect-the-dots to build up his power. The Red Tide is the lingering proof of his presence. He is connecting these points of negative energy to create a grid –

a powerful grid of evil."

"I don't get it," Lynni stated bluntly. "With all of this talk about a grids, red tides, ley lines and museums, I am thoroughly confused!"

"Hold on a minute, Lynni. I think I can show you…" Elly stood up and made her way over to the magnificent map. As she moved her hand over various push pins and silver threads strung along the length and width of the great chart. As she did this, as if by magic, the lines and cities and streets rose up from the two-dimensional graph into spectacular 3D imagery. The map came alive. AJ smiled with the satisfaction that he wasn't hallucinating.

After a brief pause to get her bearings, Elly continued to run her finger along the map. "See Lynni, this is what I think Dr. Beele is trying to explain to us. We know that Lutin is using the ley lines to travel; the silver threads on the map represent his route. The red pushpins are the portals he is using to enter and exit places from the ley line grid. These portals are located where the ley lines cross, which happen to be at specific museum sites."

"Oh, I think I get it now," Lynni exclaimed with a look of understanding. "Lutin is traveling in a grid pattern, like Dr. Beele said."

"Precisely, ladies," the curator interjected. "Fortunately for us, Lutin's grid or matrix is incomplete." Beele pointed to the map, outlining open loops in the webbed pattern of silver thread.

"What happens when the grid is finished?" Vic asked ominously.

Dr. Beele turned away from the map on the wall and faced the teens directly. He had a look of deep concern and seriousness about him. "When the grid is complete, the Nain Rouge will rule the land and water."

An eerie silence fell over the room for what seemed like an eternity.

Beele broke the tension by continuing his revelation, "The grid that Lutin is creating will tie together all of the negative energy along the ley lines. The small amounts of red tide that we have seen in these targets areas will continue to rise, grow and spread, as will all of the other natural disasters. If Lutin is able to complete his grid, he will trap us all in a giant red net of evil."

Chapter 17
The Rising Tide

Just as **Beele** finished his speech, the heavy wooden doors of the conference room blew open with great force. A strong, putrid smelling wind whipped in from the hallway, causing the group to cough and cover their eyes for protection.

"Fools!" screamed a high-pitched voice from the whirling maelstrom. The giant, magnificent map was ripped off of the wall as the teens dodged flying pushpins that seemed to bombard them from everywhere. Yards and yards of silver thread flew through the air and with deadly accuracy, wrapped themselves around the crouched figure of Dr. Beele. Again and again, the thread wound around the curator until he disappeared inside a silver cocoon.

"You think you are so wise!" screeched the voice from inside the swirling tornado, "My power is unstoppable already!"

The wind in the room was picking up, lifting pictures off of the walls and chairs off of the deep burgundy carpet. The creature could barely be seen within the cyclone of fury that brought him into the room. The pictures and chairs hung in the air for a brief, dramatic moment and then were smashed against the walls with unspeakable force. The teens huddled helplessly under the grand conference table, thankful that its heavy oaken structure was still too massive to be moved by the terrible wind.

A mournful, triumphant cry came again, "I am all-powerful! The Nain Rouge will destroy you all!"

Then, without warning, the tempest of sulphuric smoke and wind retreated out of the room and dissipated into the air. He was gone, leaving the conference room in complete shambles while the teens remained shaking in fear under the oak table.

Across the room, a muffled cry for help came from Dr. Beele's mummified remains, still wrapped in shiny silver bandages. AJ and Vic ran over to where the curator was lying and began to unravel his shiny bonds as fast as they could.

"Hold on, Dr. Beele, this will only take a minute," Vic reassured him as they removed the threads that had been wrapped around his head and face. In a moment, the museum curator could breathe freely again.

"Thank you both," Beele inhaled deeply, "I didn't get much of chance to see what all of the commotion was, but I am assuming that we all just had the displeasure of another visit from our not-so-dear friend, the Nain Rouge."

The rest of the group came over to where Dr. Beele was and helped remove the rest of the silver thread from his body. The room was a complete mess. It looked like a massive tornado had hit the conference room, leaving only destruction in its wake, while the rest of DIA offices remained untouched and intact.

"So, what are we to make of all this?" Beele stood up and asked this question aloud, directing it at no one in particular. It is clear that Lutin is gaining strength, the proof of that is scattered all around us. So, again I ask, what are we to do?"

No one said a word. What could they say? They had all seen with their own eyes how powerful Lutin had become. Tom and Elly thought back to the time where they fought the Nain Rouge and barely escaped with their lives. But now, things were different.

Lutin was free; free to wreak havoc wherever and whenever he wanted. There was no longer a curse to tie him down.

After a long period of uncomfortable silence, Elly finally spoke up. "Dr. Beele, we need help. We can't do this alone."

Vic added, "Yeah, we need to let other people know what's going on."

The curator smiled. It wasn't a happy smile, but more a smile of reassurance and understanding. "You are precisely right, both of you. A greater force than just our little, merry band will be required to stop Lutin. But I will still need help – from all of you. Let's clean this place up a bit and I will explain to you exactly what I mean."

Beele and the teenagers spent the next few minutes straightening up the conference room as best they could. As they re-attached the map to wall and discarded pieces of broken lamps, vases and wooden picture frames, they could not help but feel that a new, dangerous and exciting journey was just about to begin.

Chapter 18
The 24

Beele called down to the commissary to have refreshments brought up for his guests. He knew that once the adrenaline from Lutin's afternoon visit wore off, the children would be famished.

He guided the group back into the comfort of his office, which had been spared from Lutin's destruction. "Before we can begin this journey together," Beele began, "I need to be completely forthright and honest with all of you. To do that, I will have to reveal some personal information about me that has never been shared before."

Tom, Elly, Vic, AJ and Lynni continued to eat their cucumber and chicken salad sandwiches, but chewed much more slowly, as their attentions were drawn to the weighty words of the mysterious curator.

"In just a few short months," Beele began, "I will be gathering with my fellow knights from around the world. These meetings, which will be taking place around the country will culminate in a final battle with the Nain Rouge; at least that is what I suppose will happen… We can never be too sure about these sorts of things."

"OK Doc," Vic spat out between large bites of cherry cobbler; "What the heck are you talking about? I'm completely lost."

"Again, I am sorry," Dr. Beele blushed slightly and cleared his throat, "I seemed to have gotten ahead of myself again. One thing this journey will require is complete and full disclosure. I intend for all of you to know all about me before you make your decision whether or not to join me on this once-in-a-lifetime adventure."

The teens stared back and forth at each other, looking around for some sign of logic or reason. It was useless. No one could figure out what the curator what talking about. However, they knew that if they waited long enough, all would be revealed. So, without interruption, they each made the silent decision to let Beele finish what he had to say, regardless of his stops and starts.

"As I was saying," Beele began again, "Complete disclosure. It is important for all of you to know that I am one of the 24. The twenty-four knights of Sir Gawain's Most Noble Order of the Garter."

With that brief announcement, Hieronymus walked back to desk drawer, opened it, and removed a small, forest green felt-covered jewelry box. He opened the box and lifted a large blue and gold-enameled medallion from the silk-lined box.

"The medal!" Tom and Elly shouted at the same time. It was a medallion very similar to one that had fallen out of one of Dr. Beele's books almost two years before. It was also the same sort of badge they had seen dangling from the curator's costume on the night they battled Lutin for the first time.

The medallion depicted a magnificent knight, decked in blue armor, on horseback, slaying a green dragon with his extended lance. Around the border of the badge were the words:

"Honi soit qui mal y pense"

The curator handed the large pin to Elly, who passed it around to Vic, AJ, Lynni and eventually Tom. Each one of them perused the shiny figure, running their fingers along the gilded lance and armor, while lingering over the strange words along the border of the golden badge.

"So then, you are a real knight!" Elly blurted out while the others remained intrigued with Dr. Beele's artifact. "I knew it from the first time you told us the story of the Order of the Garter."

"Yes, it is true," Beele began. "Of course, there is a bit more information that I failed to share with you. I purposely did not disclose the mission and charter of our order. Since King Edward III of England founded our order in 1348, we have been sworn to protect any land in which we dwell from the manifestation of evil. There have always been only 24 of us since our founding. When one of us dies, another is chosen to take our place.

The Knights of the Garter have been aware of the Nain Rouge for centuries. We have battled his dark deeds and malicious forces across many continents since the time of St. George. Normally, we keep our activities quiet, acting in secrecy to avoid disturbing the everyday worlds of ordinary people. But the times have changed; and with change comes the requirement for support from those outside of our order."

"So, you want us to help you fight Lutin?" AJ asked inquisitively.

"This very group, all of you, in fact." Beele responded directly. "There are a number of Knights of the Garter right here, scattered about North America. A few are museum curators, just like me. Our task will be to join with these men and women to stop Lutin before he completes his negative energy grid."

"I'm in." Vic spoke without hesitation, "When do we leave?"

"Not so fast, young man," Beele gently chided; "I will need to make travel preparations to secure our safe passage. All of you will need to gain permission from your parents. I am confident that your impending spring holidays from school will give us ample time to complete our journey, as well as our mission."

The discussion that followed between the group was both spirited and anxious. The curator had disclosed all of the details of his previous journey and how he had notified all of the knights from around the country.

As the late afternoon melted into the low, purple evening, Hieronymus instructed the teens to return home and explain everything to their parents and family. He made is very clear that there were to be no secrets kept from their families, as Lutin would feed off of any deceit or dishonesty from within the group. They had all agreed to go with the curator. In many ways, they felt that they had no choice. No matter what happened, they had agreed to stick together - no one was willing to break such a sacred pact.

Chapter 19
Minus One

The *week flew* by rapidly, like thickening clouds pushed across the sky by an approaching storm. Tom, Elly, Vic, AJ and Lynni tried to maintain some sense of normalcy at school, but they all failed miserably. No one could concentrate on their schoolwork with thoughts of good and evil swinging like subconscious pendulums inside their heads.

Spring Break was only a few days away. At lunch, the teens met at their usual spot near the student commons area. Everyone was there except for Lynni.

"So, did you guys get everything settled with your mom and dad?" Tom asked the group.

"I told them everything, like Dr. Beele said," AJ answered.

Vic added, "Yeah, at first my parents didn't believe me. My dad even called down to the DIA to make sure that Beele wasn't some nut job or something. But after a long conversation, they agreed. You have to admit, it does sound crazy; chasing a psychopathic troll around the country trying to save the world."

"Our parents were just happy that we finally leveled with them," Elly said. "Tom and I had kept all of this stuff quiet for so long; it was such a relief to let our family know what was going on. I was always afraid that they would think I was crazy or even worse, stuck in some emotional, teenage fantasy. I'm just glad that they didn't laugh and that they're letting me go on this trip."

As the band of adventurers was talking, they could see Lynni running toward them from across the commons. Her head was down as she ran, with her hair flying wildly from side to side. In a moment, Lynni stood in front of them, her eyes red and puffy from the tears that stained her pale cheeks.

"What's wrong Lynni?" Elly asked with deep concern, as she got up and put her arm around her friend.

"M-m-my mom and dad…th-th-they won't let me go…" A hush fell over the group.

"Why Lynni, why can't you go?" Tom asked with a gentle, calm voice.

Lynni gathered herself a little and blotted the black eyeliner streaks that ran down her face. "I told them everything, everything. I told them the truth about what happened at the secret tunnel. I told them about the power grid. I even told them all about the Nain Rouge. They just sat there and listened. They didn't say a word for an hour… then they told me I wasn't going…"

Lynni started to cry again. Elly held her tighter and the rest of the teens gathered more closely around her, shielding Lynni from the prying eyes of the other lunch goers. After she gathered herself once more, Lynni explained that her parents believed everything – just like her friends. Only their belief backfired. Because they believed what their daughter had told them, Lynni's parents knew how dangerous the spring break journey would be and refused to let her go. All the begging and pleading in the world would not make them change their minds. Even a visit from Dr. Beele could not make Lynni's parents budge. They decided that their daughter had been through enough stress and trauma and they were not willing to put her in harm's way again. The answer was "NO" and that was final.

As the teens listened to Lynni, the realization that they would be setting out on their adventure without Lynni began to set in. The final lunch bell rang, signaling the end of the period and the beginning of a new one. Tom, Elly, AJ, Vic and Lynni gathered up their empty bags and apple cores and headed off toward the main hall, together, for at least a little while longer.

Chapter 20
The Silent Embarking

S*pring break had* finally arrived and Tom had all of his gear in a pile at the bottom of the stairs. A duffel bag, a back pack and his sleeping bag would be the only equipment he would carry in a week long journey across the country. Dr. Beele had instructed the teens to meet him in the high school parking lot just before dawn.

Tom's parents were up long before he was. They were sitting at the kitchen table talking when Tom came in to say goodbye. Thankfully, his mom and dad did not get too emotional. Tom knew that if his mom started crying, it would set him off and then he might just lose his nerve to leave the house. No, in a strange way, his parents knew that this trip involved something that Tom was destined to do. He had been through so much already and they just wanted some closure for him. Sure, his parents were scared, but they knew Tom was growing up and that in life, there were some battles that had to be faced head on. This was Tom's fight and they would have to be content to sit on the sidelines and hope and pray for the best.

Similar scenes were being played out in other houses around town. Elly, AJ and Vic were all gathering their supplies and equipment and saying goodbye to their families.

At AJ's house, Pip kept blocking the door, trying to keep AJ from leaving. She knew that there was danger beyond the door and she wanted to protect her best friend in any way she could. AJ scooted the little Westie away from the front door and made his way down the driveway and into the street.

The high school parking lot was as empty and dark as it could be. The black top surface seemed to absorb the night, reflecting only darkness against the cloud-covered sky. The four teenagers met on Crooks Road and headed north past Thirteen Mile. The only light came from the blinking yellow traffic signal and the dim headlights of a newspaper van, making its way toward its early morning deliveries.

Though it was just before six o'clock in the morning, the dawn seemed to be hours and miles away. No one said a word. Maybe, it was because they were all so groggy from the lack of sleep. Maybe, it was just plain fear that no one was willing to share. There was an ominous loneliness that enveloped the adventurers as they turned down Lexington Boulevard, heading into the school parking lot. It was the feeling one might have approaching the dark edge of a cliff; looking down into the inky unknown, wondering what it would feel like to fall that far down.

As the teens stood shivering in the pre-dawn morning, they realized how much they missed Lynni. Though she could be a pain sometimes, she was kind, loyal and always a great friend. Thoughts of Lynni served only to fuel their anxiety and depression, as the cold wrapped around their winter jackets, creeping underneath the cracks and crevices of their nylon skins.

Two headlights bounced up and down into the empty parking lot. The group could make out the faint outline of a gray Ford Econoline van. As the vehicle lurched toward them, they could read, "Detroit Institute of Arts", on the side of the large panel van.

The vehicle circled around the teenagers and stopped directly in front of them. After a brief moment, the driver's side door opened and Dr. Hieronymus Beele stepped down from the running board. With the door wide open, the teens could smell the warm and inviting scent of hot chocolate. Beele stood before them now, holding a cardboard tray of Styrofoam cups filled with steaming hot cocoa. The smile that spread across his face was contagious. Soon, everyone was sipping their hot drinks, chatting and loading up the back of the van with various sleeping bags, duffels and backpacks.

Once the van was fully packed, Dr. Beele explained that their first stop would be Chicago, where they were to meet with a fellow knight from the order. The mood had changed for the better now. There seemed to be a revived sense of excitement as the vehicle began its final turn out of the parking lot and into Lexington Boulevard.

"Dr. Beele, stop!" Elly shouted without warning from the back bench seat.

Beele slammed on the brakes, jerking the van to an abrupt halt. Elly stood up quickly and pointed dramatically out of the side window.

From the window, the entire vanload of adventurers stared in wonder at a figure moving rapidly across the baseball diamonds toward the school parking lot. As the dark shadow grew closer, Tom, Elly, Vic, AJ and Dr. Beele could begin to make out a familiar shape emerging from the mist that still hung in the grassy outfield.

As two fast-moving legs sped across the parking lot toward the van, a collection of smiles and raised eyebrows filled every side window of the gray vehicle. In spontaneous unison, the van erupted with cheers,

"Lynni! It's Lynni!"

It was Lynni, coming closer and closer to them, with a sleeping bag in one arm and her powder blue duffle bag dangling from her other shoulder. She lumbered into the side door of the waiting van, breathless but smiling from ear to ear.

As the van began its forward motion again, you could hear the muffled chattering and excitement from all of the teens. Now there was full confidence that their adventure had begun in earnest. The whole team was now intact.

The End

Made in the USA
Charleston, SC
11 March 2015